The First Book of Mimi

Daniel Aldouby

Published by The Pelican Communications Group

ISBN-10: 1499116349
ISBN-13: 978-1499116342

DEDICATION

This book is dedicated to my family, whose love and support made this book possible. In particular, to my long-suffering and patient wife Barbara; my two daughters Sharon and Marcie, who taught me that daughters have a strength different from men, and can be more brilliant than their fathers; to David, my son, who has shown me love and patience which few fathers earn, and is just a lovable, middle-aged puppy; and to the rest of the family for having put up with my puns and jokes ad infinitum. That goes double for my six grandchildren.

ACKNOWLEDGMENTS

I am grateful for the memory of my Father and Mother, and for my brother Lee, because of our kitchen table arguments, debates, and jokes, which helped to prepare me for a verbal life; my elementary teachers at schools 18 and 16 and the librarians on Madison Avenue in Elizabeth, NJ; who gave me a voracious appetite for books; Rabbis Arthur Hertzberg, Joachim Prinz, and Howard Hersch, who helped me to appreciate the beauty of the study of religion and its history; my English Lit teachers at Rutgers University-Newark, who helped me to love the beauty of the English Language; my students at Rutgers University Osher-All Life Learning Classes, who provided the challenge to learn more, so that I could keep up with their curiosity and interest. Last but not least, I am grateful to that unknown woman from Australia who wrote to me at care2.com and who put me up to writing this tale.

PROLOGUE

I must apologize to the reader, for there will be some confusion when reading the following tale. You see, I have had more than one life, lived in many cultures, and learned quite a few languages; sometimes, I forget to stay in the character I was at the time of whatever event or life is being described. Nevertheless, the truth of my lives' journeys will nullify all of the verbal glitches, which mar the smooth procession of the telling. I beg your indulgence.

Thank you.

Mimi

IN MY BEGINNING

My birth name was Batya. It means "daughter from god." My father died before I was born, and so my mother was grateful that I came along. With my mother and two older brothers, we managed to survive on a little patch of ground on the shores of Kinneret — the lake that looks like a harp, and that is what the name means. It nestles in the Jordan River valley of Galil. Life was not all bad, and sometimes it was good, especially when we went swimming or just sat and talked. We went to Jerusalem, of course, on the required pilgrimages, but I did not like the mobs and the noise.

Hundreds of years later, after the Syrians had left and the Romans had arrived, the mobs and noise did not grow still. It was only after the destruction that the stillness came. Then a few hundred years after that, building started on the hills of our once-golden city — first some churches, on top of the rubble, and after that, mosques on the Temple Mount. I saw it all. You see, I am not what I am, but another. Here is how it happened.

It was the time after the priest of Modin, Matityahu, and his five sons rebelled against the Syrian-Greco way of living. There was turmoil throughout the land. The Temple had been profaned, and the people were up in arms against the oppressor.

I was washing laundry at the lake. The day was warm, not hot, and a gentle breeze kept me comfortable. I saw a cloudless sky, birds flying or nesting, and thought that I should like to live like this for a long time — in peace, quiet, marrying in the future and settling down here, near Ima and my brothers. As I daydreamed, visions of the future darted through my head; then clouds appeared, and the sky grew dark. There was no rain, but there was thunder and lightning all around me. Suddenly, there was a stillness, which only a moonless night can bring, yet it was mid-morning. I heard a voice, small and still, and it spoke my name.

"Batya, Batya."

I looked but saw no one, so I did not reply. Again I heard,

"Batya, Batya"

I was frightened, because I knew that my ears had heard my name, but there was no one to be seen. So I whispered, "Who is it? Who, who?" In Hebrew, it is "Mi ze? Mi, Mi"? That is the language I spoke in those days.

And the voice answered, "I am the same who spoke to Moses, who has given you the law and has kept you alive. I see wickedness and injustice in high places. You know not of this, except the noise of which you complain. You have been chosen to speak my words to the people. In return for this work, you shall be recompensed with life exceeding that of Methuselah of old. You must use only words that the people will understand, for they will not see me, lest they know me and they die. You, at eighteen years of age, are a woman, and people who are ignorant of me and my word may ignore and try to deny those things of which you speak, but I shall be with you, and they will know that you speak with the voice of the prophet. You may think that you would not like to do this and that marriage and children is your choice. This may very well be in your future; however, your destiny is to speak to my people to help them seek the right road in life. Now, what say you?"

I raised my eyes and saw the bright blue color of the sky, mirrored in the waters of Kinneret, felt the breeze on my face, and yet saw no presence other than myself. So I said nothing. A bolt of lightning split the water, and a wave, taller than I rushed at me, and stopped as if a wall stood at my face. I knew then that I must answer, and so I said, "What would you have of me? What have I done to reap this reward, not having sown the seeds of ambition — or is it a punishment for some ignoble transgression? Have I done some enormous wrong to others or to thee? Why me? Why?"

And the voice answered again, whispering, "Because the Universe demands your services. Because you have been chosen; because you shall be the voice of supreme justice, mercy, compassion, and will help the growth of a great humanity. Now, go home, and prepare for traveling. You have much work to do, and it will take many lifetimes to accomplish all that awaits you. Today, when the sun is lowering and evening comes, pack, sleep, and, in the morning, bid your family farewell, and I shall further instruct you as you leave. Go now, for I am with you."

Yes, I was trembling with awe and some fear, yet those final words echoing Abraham's experience and David's song did comfort me. I went home, packed my few belongings and laid them aside, saying nothing of the happenings by the water. We ate, and, at dark, I slept, dreamlessly, which was amazing, given my state of emotional and physical fear and apprehension.

When the morning dawned, we arose and ate together, and, when I told Ima and my brothers that I must leave, they objected, they argued, they wept, and they admonished me not to desert them. I could not tell them what had happened, but I did tell them that my leaving had to do with having to fulfill a vow and go to the city, alone. Trembling with grief and sorrow, Ima told me of the dangers of a single woman walking on the road and warned me of the pitfalls of loneliness. Avram, my elder brother, told Ima that he would accompany me, but I told him that it was not to be, for I must do this for myself. At the end, they saw that there was nothing they could say or do which would prevent me from my mission, and so they kissed me and bade me a peaceful and safe journey. With sadness surrounding me, I left.

I FIND A PROTECTOR

The sun was behind me and to the east, so I walked the shore road to the south and followed it. As I walked, my mind told me to believe that I would be guarded, yet I feared for a future which I knew not. As the sun rose and heated the air, I rested under the shade of some fruit trees, and, as I rested, a man came to the grove to see to his orchard. When he saw me, he looked at me with intense eyes and then asked "And what is this comely maiden doing? Are you waiting for me?"

"Nay, adoni," I replied. "I am going to the City of David, and there I hope to fulfill whatever the Lord wills of me."

"And do you know what our Lord wills of you, my pretty pomegranate?"

He asked this with a smile on his face and a not-so-kindly voice. He approached me and put out his hand as if to touch my hair.

Before he could finish his reach, there was a crack of lightning from out of the blue sky, and, next to him, the lightning opened a smoking pit. He stared at the pit, and at me, turned, and ran rather quickly back whence he had come. I looked around. No one was there, and I muttered to myself, "That was not bad, my Lord. In fact, I know now that thou guardest me."

Again, that voice came to me, except that it did not sound as soothing as before, saying, "Enough of the classical thees and thous!" We shall be together, you and I, for centuries to come and so we must use understandable, non-formal language. As you will discover in the future, that kind of language is convenient for separating people one from the other. You shall from now on address me either as "Ya" when you are excited and when speaking directly to me, and when you tell others of me, you shall use the name Ayl Elyon — "Ruler on High" or some other fancy name, whatever comes to your mind. It really makes no difference to me, for I know who I am. Is that understood? In return, I shall not call you 'Batya,' for you are no longer a little girl daughter, and you are certainly not my begotten daughter. I prefer to call you 'Mimi,' for that was the first utterance of yours when we first were acquainted. And when people ask who you are, you shall answer 'Mimi' or 'Mimi Ehyeh' — for you shall be my voice — 'Mimi Who Shall Be.'"

I nodded — and the voice suddenly took up once more, "…And why do you only nod? Are you not satisfied with your name? Do you wish a miracle as you receive my gift? Why a nod? Why not a gracious 'Thank you'? What ails you?"

I looked up and down and right and left, and saw no one. I then closed my eyes and whispered, "I cannot see you. I do not know what you want from me. I have had the same name for eighteen years, and it suited me well. I am accustomed to it, and, just like that, you come along and change it completely. Do you think that this is just? Is it fair that you play with me like this?"

"So," said Ya, "the girl rebels. The princess is discomfited, is irritable, and dislikes higher authority. There will come a time when you will hear of a person named Job, and you shall enquire of his life and afflictions, and then you shall know how kindly I have dealt with you, Mimi. Now, swallow your grief, and know that your name will be famous throughout the dwellings of humanity, and yours will be a reputation of renown. Did you forget that your new name also includes part of my answer to Moses when he inquired of who I was? Are you not satisfied to bear not only a self-spoken name but also a biblical reference as to your identity? Know who you are, woman! You have become the verbal sword of your creator. With your mouth shall all humans learn my goal. You shall be a teacher, a whip, a way of showing a true returning to righteousness. That is your reason for being here. This is to be your existence and life. Remember this. Now, keep walking, and I shall soon acquaint you with your work, and I shall guide you."

And so I walked southward. The sun rose higher, and the heat melted my sinews. I walked on. Then I noticed a woman, standing at a well. I approached, bid her a peaceful day, and asked if I might assuage my thirst. She readily agreed, and, within a short while, we were talking as if we had known each other for years. She told me that she and her husband had a small garden and orchard, along with some beasts for milk and burden, as well as meat, when necessary. I told her of my going southward to fulfill a mission-vow. When she heard that, she asked me whether I was truly a daughter of Jacob — or one of those Greek life lovers. When I told her that I was a descendant of Hosea and a devout worshipper of the People of God, she took me by the hand and walked with me to her home. She took me in, fed me a wonderful meal, and then took me to the pasture. Leaving me at the pasture gate, she entered and came back with a young donkey and told me that this donkey was named "Tembel," a term which means "simpleton," or "idiot." Her husband had no use for this donkey because it would not pull a small plow or bear him for travel. She told me, as she blanketed the animal and put a rope on him to rein him in, that he was now mine and that I should try to mount the beast as transport. I walked to the front of the animal, looked it in the eye, and whispered, "It's not your fault. I guess Ayl has a job for you. I tell you that I shall try to be kind to you and treat you well. But you must not begrudge the burden of my weight on your back, for you also have a mission, my friend."

The animal stood still, not moving. One would think that it was thinking of a counter-offer. Finally, it turned its eyes to me, nodded once, and I knew we were to be good traveling companions. I then, on the spot, renamed him Yofi, because I thought him to be the prettiest donkey I had ever met. I think he liked it, because whenever I mentioned his name, his ears would rise, and he would answer.

Yofi and I bade goodbye to the kind woman and set off southward. Every once in a while, as the road bent toward Kinneret, I would stop for a while, let Yofi drink and graze, and then continue. He liked it also when, as we were on the road, I would sing some of David's songs to him. There were other songs, composed by the Levites, which he loved, especially the one about praising Ya, which has the line, "Let the whole soul praise him," for every time I sang the line, he would bray. You know, of course, that, in English the words "bray" and "pray" are very similar in spelling and phonetically. There is not much difference — just one letter separates man from donkey. Finally we came to Bet Shahn. I had finished about one third of my journey.

I SLEEP AND WAKE IN A TOWN

Entering Bet Shahn, I asked a passing woman if there was an inn or place to stay for the night. She pointed straight ahead and told me that it was not too far in that direction. Thanking her, Yofi and I plodded on. When we came to a place, which looked a little bigger than the rest of the small homes, we went into the courtyard and saw that there was a pretty garden and a fenced-in place for donkeys and goats. I walked through an open door and spoke to a man I believed to be the innkeeper. He told me that, unfortunately, there was no room for a woman, because the few rooms were already filled with men for the night. However, he did offer to lend me a place near the animals, which was a small hut for his plow and other unrecognizable things. I paid him and, taking Yofi with me, went to set my private room in order. After telling Yofi not to make noise, I tied him to a staff in the ground, and bade him *lyla tov* — good night. I lit my small oil lamp and stepped into the hut. I could not earnestly say that it was a clean, well-lighted place, for it was not clean, although cracks in the ceiling did let in some moonlight. However, one has to make do with that which one has. So, I dropped my cloak to the ground, lay my head down, thanked Ya for an eventful and safe day, and slept.

At the appearance of daylight, with the piercing screech of a nearby rooster claiming his portion of the earth, I awoke, greeted the day, stretched, and, feeling tired, went back to sleep. I had slept for a short while, when a loud bray awoke me. Yofi was hungry, thirsty, and lonely. As I went out, Yofi stopped braying and stood, waiting. I watered him and released him to graze, while I attended to my morning rituals. As I finished my ablutions, a voice spoke up enquiringly, saying "Peace unto you, fair maiden. What now?"

I looked and saw a rather comely man, a little older than I, smiling at me. "What now what?" I answered.

"Do you plan on staying in Bet Shahn, or are you traveling?" he questioned.

"I am on a mission-vow to the city of David and plan to leave momentarily."

His face brightened as he said, "Ah, so you head south on the Salt Sea Road. I am heading southerly also, but further than the Holy City. Perhaps we can travel together so that we can converse and hasten our feeling of time."

I did not know how to reply. Ya had not informed me of the possibility of this meeting with such a charming man. I was confused. As I hesitated, Yofi stepped up to the man and licked his face. I knew then that this might be a sign, and, chancing it, I said, "I agree that two people make better conversation than one. Allow me to breakfast, and we shall depart."

And so, we left Bet Shahn, the four of us — for Nahtahn (that was his name) also had a donkey. As we headed south, he told me of his life, having been born in the far north, where the river begins, and having learned the leather trade, he was traveling toward the south, hoping to find nomads and others, who needed sandals and other leather goods. I told him about Ima and my brothers, and my former happy life, and so the time passed quickly, and another afternoon was ending. There was no city or town or people to be found, so we camped by the road, I lying down next to Yofi and Nahtahn next to Hamor, his donkey. I could not sleep for a while, thinking of this man, going to sleep almost within reach — the first time this had ever happened to me in all my life. It was an odd yet interesting time, having ideas and feelings passing through my being, things and ideas which had, at times come fleetingly through the years and then vanished and which now crowded my thoughts. Yet, I thrust them aside, and, nestling toward Yofi's warmth, I slept.

THE START OF THE THIRD DAY

We awoke with the arrival of sunrise and were quickly on the way, for we knew we would soon be passing through Jericho and that my journey would end by nightfall. As we went southward, again, we talked of the marvels of Jerusalem of old, and how Solomon's kingdom had grown since the days of the Jebusites and then how the nation had split and how Israel had been vanquished, leaving the tribes of Judah and Binyamin in the south. Nahtahn opined that he did not like the idea of making all fit males go to Lebanon to fell Cedar trees for the building of the Temple and then levying a temple tax, once it had been built. He thought that Solomon had taxed the working people too much, in order to support his family and army and horses, and that there was too much taxation on those who could not afford it. He also mentioned that there had been grumbling throughout the land, especially in the northern hills and plains where the 10 tribes had settled, about the conquest of Jerusalem, and how they, who had been in the van of the fighting, were the last in the triumphant entrance of David into his new Capitol. I listened and wondered what this was all about.

David's reign had ended more than eight hundred years ago. The ten tribes of Israel were nowhere to be seen, and my brothers, being young, had not been called for any labors, and we had not had any tax collectors visit us. I thought that perhaps Nahtahn was grumbling because he could as yet find no work. It was not until later that I found that Nahtahn had been referring to events which happened after Solomon's death. And so, the day passed, and, as we passed Jericho, we marveled at the rubble upon which it was built. Later that afternoon, we came through a pass in the hills and saw Jerusalem in the distance, gleaming in the late sunlight. As we drew nearer, I said to myself, "Thank you, Ya. You have provided transport, friendship and an easy trip for me. Now I can see the City of David, and it is truly a wonderment. Thank you."

As if in answer, far off in the distance, we saw a rainbow arch from one end of the horizon to the other. This was amazing, since the rainy season was still far off. One usually does not see rainbows in the dry season. Nahtahn remarked on this, saying "I cannot believe that which I see. Never have I witnessed a rainbow during this time of the year. Do you see it also, Mimi?"

I answered that I did, and we just looked and watched, together, as the rainbow slowly vanished, leaving the horizon broken only by hilltops. We moved on, and as we approached the gates of the City, Nahtahn spoke. "I shall be staying for a day, to see if I can find some work. Shall I be seeing you? Will you be safe? Do you wish to spend some of our time together, so that we can be assured of each other's well-being? For my part, I would prefer that we did."

I alighted from Yofi and said, "I shall move into the shade of that tree and think on this. When I return, I shall know the answer."

HOPEFUL ADVICE

I left and sat on a boulder under the tree and pondered. Finally, I whispered, "All right, Ya. You have provided me with a fine specimen of a protector. I think he is adorable and do not know what you wish me to do. I think that if there are any more feelings and thoughts as I had last night, things will happen very quickly. What shall I do? What shall I say? Please counsel me." It started to rain. I did not need miracles. I needed advice and whispered once more. "Listen, Ya. Do not play merrily with my feelings. I was civil in my questioning. Is not the Lord of Creation a civil Being?"

The rain stopped. The still, small voice spoke. "Sorry about that, Mimi. I did not mean to rain on your tirade. Here is your answer. I have plans for Nahtahn. He must go south to continue for a time his venture. But, he will return, at your suggestion. Tell him that you must complete your mission at this time and that, if he wishes, he may meet you at this same gate one fortnight from the next new moon. The morning after the full moon appears and indicates mid-month, he is to meet you. Is that understood?"

I smiled. "Yes Ya. I understand completely. But tell me. Is Nahtahn my intended? Is he to be my betrothed?"

The answer came quickly. "Hush. You may have the blood of the prophets running in your veins, but it does not mean that you must know your own future. Do your work as I have said. You will be what you will be."

And so, I returned to face Nahtahn, and told him that I would meet him in six weeks, on the morning after the fortnight after the New Moon Proclamation. After a discussion of what that meant, we both understood the timing of that meeting, and, then, he looked at me in puzzlement and, without questioning said, "Then I shall leave now, so that I can be done with my business and return in time for our meeting. I shall see you here at the gate at the dawning of the appointed time. But, I tell you, Mimi, you are a puzzling, although beauteous, intelligent, and fascinating person, and I have much admiration for you. Shalom, *Uvrachah*. Peace and fullness, and may you be blessed." And he turned, and, following around the walls of the city, he left.

My heart felt as if it had turned to a rock of salt. Tears came to my eyes as I saw his image dwindle in the distance, and I felt lonely as I had never felt before. Again, that voice summoned me to my task.

"Mimi. Time for work! Leave Yofi here, tied to the donkey post, and go within the city gates, where you will see the public square. Wait there, and I shall speak further at that time. Now *Yallah*, Go."

STILL NOON OF THE THIRD DAY

On hearing this, I entered the city. The place was crowded with people selling things, food, people arguing, and others just waving their arms and shouting. There was no quiet space, no peacefulness about this area. I did not know what to say or do. I stood and wondered how anything could get done, given the amount of noise. Seeing a woman standing alone, selling what appeared to be vegetables she had grown, I approached her and asked her what was going on.

"It is now the second day of the week. Where do you come from? Don't you know that the Tora is read aloud in the marketplace so that all the people know the law? It is also read on the fifth day of the week. How can you know how to live, if you don't know the law? Where are you from, that you didn't know that the market takes place on only these days?"

As my face turned red with this rebuke, I thought of Ya and his failure to warn me of pitfalls along the way. I faced the woman and, in my most polite voice said, "You must pardon me, for I am a simple country girl from the Lake District and do not know the ways of the city. Does this happen wherever there is a marketplace?"

"Everywhere in which the children of Jacob live, daughter. And how do you study the law?" she enquired.

"Well, I don't really study it. My Ima told me stories about Jacob and the tribes, and Moses, and what we women have to do to be ritually pure, but I do not know all the laws. Do you?"

The woman laughed. "You're a sprightly young lioness. How old are you? Are you married? Betrothed? Looking for a husband? I have a nephew who will be twenty four, a little big around the middle, but a good man, and a hard worker. Perhaps you would like to meet him."

"I'm sorry. You see, I am on a kind of pilgrimage mission and do not have time for social activities, as I must keep my vow."

"A vow!" she exclaimed, with a quick intake of breath. "I did not know it was as serious a matter as that. One does not make vows lightly. I have seldom met someone who has done that. I did not think people did that any more. Can you tell me about it? What does it entail?"

I eyed her, waited, and said, "That I cannot discuss with you; however, I do not take vows lightly. I have never done this before."

"Well then, I shall not keep you from your mission. I will only wish you all that is best for you, and may the Lord be with you."

I thanked her politely and wandered further in the public square. I smiled to myself, knowing that her wish for me had already been granted. But yet, I did not know what it is that Ya wanted me to do now. Here I was, in Yerushalayim, the City of David, wistfully thinking of Nahtahn and his broad shoulders and curly hair, and with nothing to do but wait. I saw a small niche in the wall, which must have belonged to one of the merchants. It was empty. I stepped in, turned to the wall, closed my eyes, and whispered, "Ya,

Ya, are you here? If you are, please take a moment of your time and be patient with me. I long to know why I am here. Where must I go? What must I do? I cannot wander like this for a month and a half. Please give me an answer — sooner and not later. I need to know now." And I waited.

I SHOULD HAVE EATEN LUNCH

As I waited, I was able to see, not far away from my niche, a raised platform of stone. On this platform stood a man, bearded, with hands waving here and there. He seemed to be speaking to a small crowd of onlookers. As I tried to concentrate on this scene, the whole square became as still and dark as midnight. I saw nor heard no one, no beast, no sound at all. "Oh, come now Ya. Is this the right thing to do — play tricks with me? I addressed you very politely, and then you darken my world and deafen my ears. What kind of a protector does this to a maiden? I am ashamed of you. Really I am. I thought better of you."

The darkness was so intense that I could not see my hand in front of me. The silence was so great yet, despite my deafness, I could hear my heart beat. And then, I got my answer —

"You listen to me, Mimi! Why do you think it is dark and quiet? I have cloaked you this way, so that we may address each other without interruption. By the way, haven't you been taught how to address your creator? What is wrong with you, girl?"

"If I have offended you, Ya, please forgive me. But you must realize that Ima never imagined that someday, I would be conversing with you, and so she did not teach me the proper words to do this, if those words really exist. I find this mission business not only puzzling, but also tiring and drawn out. Cannot you, as the Creator and the Almighty and all of that — can't you just do this mission quickly by your own self? Why do you need an eighteen-year-old to accomplish this task?"

"Oh Mimi, Mimi. Forgive me if I laugh, for I have not enjoyed a human being such as you since I had a lengthy argument with Avraham. But that is why you are here. You are basically acting as an advocate. You see, if I were to appear to the people and speak directly to them, it would be so awesome and awful, that they would die on the spot. I need a messenger, Mimi, and you are the one I have chosen."

YA AND I TALK FURTHER

When I heard that I was to be a messenger, I wondered who would be the recipient of Ya's message and what the message was about. So, once more, I questioned, "…and who, my Good Ya, might be the recipient of that message, and would it not be good and proper for you to tell me, exactly, what the contents of that message would be? It is difficult for me to discuss something of which I am ignorant. It is now the third day of our acquaintance, and yet I struggle with lack of knowing."

"Well petitioned, good servant," said Ya, "and I am glad that you are aware of your limitations, for the task I shall lay on you is hard and seemingly perilous, for the message will not be welcome. The recipients are the people of the city, from highest to lowest. No one is exempt from it. All must know of it. You shall speak the words which I place on your tongue. No matter what you see or hear, when you speak, nothing will stop you from delivering my message. Is that clear?"

I pondered this, for I had heard the word "peril" and thought "danger." What did this mean? I knew no one here except for one woman, and now I felt foreboding for myself. Then the voice continued—

"Now, now, have a little faith. Did I not tell you that you would be protected? Why do you fear for your safety? Look around you. All you see is dark. All you hear is my voice. Where is danger for you in the darkness? First, I shall make it light. Then I shall restore the tumult. But before I do, here is your task. When all is restored as before, you will approach the bearded man who was speaking on the platform. When he pauses, you will mount the platform, and while he is collecting his thoughts, you will raise your both arms high, and say the following, "Thus says the Lord, who brought you out of Egypt, who gave you the two tablets of stone, who gave you this sweet land as your inheritance. I am the one who breathed life into the world and gave you what you deserve. Now and here I will speak of Justice, both of here and wherever you dwell. Hear me, my people, for I do not wish evil upon you." There was a slight pause and then, "Mimi, can you remember that? Raise both arms high and those words. Can you remember?"

MY FIRST PUBLIC SPEECH EVER

I closed my eyes. I did not have to, since there was nothing to see. I thought about the words I had heard and saw them in my mind.

"Look, Ya, I can see those words in my head right now. I do not know if they will come out as we wish, but I know, from my few days with you, that you will not leave me speechless and dumb when I go to do your bidding. So, let us be off and get done with it. I am ready."

The darkness vanished, and there was light; the quiet became the noise of trade, gossip, argumentation, and joking. I almost preferred the quiet and darkness but knew that I had to step out of my niche. I walked slowly to where the bearded man was holding forth and listened. He was talking about whether it was time to lift the law of mixing flax and wool for garments. He discussed the economic hurt to the clothing industry, the need for updating the law, and for doing away with all these laws, which were weighing on the people, especially the merchants. As he stopped to draw in his breath, I walked up the step leading to the platform and joined him. I raised my arms, opened my mouth, and spoke.

There was a sudden silence as I started uttering the words assigned, and the silence spread as a circle of waves made by a stone thrown into a pond. As I finished the last word, there was a stirring in the crowd, and, suddenly, when I had uttered the word "evil" and finished the last sentence, a man, dressed in finery, jumped up on the platform and, after confronting me, shouted,

"Who are you woman, that you dare address the people of the city in such an imperious voice? By what leave do you have the temerity to rebuke and speak blasphemy? We know you not, nor do we accept your words. Begone, blasphemer, lest we bring you to trial and assure that you live a very short life."

This frightened me. Never had I been addressed in this manner. But I had nothing to fear, for at the moment when he mentioned the word "life," he fell in a swoon and lay there as if dead. Two more men, with whom he had stood, immediately jumped onto the platform and lunged at me. I was paralyzed with fear and moved not. As they were about to put their hands on me, they also fell into a swoon, and I felt my voice return and my mouth open. I felt very comfortable with myself, and words began to flow from my lips. I was amazed, more so than the people who were witnessing the event. Then a voice came thundering from within me. I felt its strength and power, and it reached to every corner of the market square and beyond. I was as another spectator, astonished at myself. But at least I knew what was happening. Ya was coming through for me, and I was prophesying.

YA AND I CONTINUE OUR SPEECH

"Ye have heard that the law be done away with. Ye have heard that the law brings hardships. Ye have heard that the law is too old to mean anything in these latter times. Have not the sages interpreted these laws to you whenever you questioned? Did they not tell you that there are some laws which have no practical application, except to remind you of who you once were and who you are now? Today you have heard of Shatnis. The speaker has questioned the worth of this law. He says that tailors suffer because of this law, that clothing is priced high because of this law, and that this law may have been good for another time but is worthless for now. Let me reason with you. Did I not set you apart from the pagans to be a holy nation of priests? Did I not tell you to separate the Sabbath from all the other days of the week? Why to do this? I shall tell you. First I myself rested on the Sabbath. So the sages wrote. Another reason — and just as important — is because you were slaves to the Pharaoh. Ponder this: Do slaves have a Shabbat? Do slaves have time to ponder, to reason, to think about who they are, what they are, and what they could be? No! Only the Shabbat set human beings free, free to study, free to think of things other than commerce and work and those other unnecessary cluttering of the mind. You are free because the Sabbath keeps you free. The Sabbath reminds you of the separation of slavery and freedom. Thus it is with Shatnis — you separate the flax from the wool to remember the separation of yourselves from idol worshippers and yourselves from slavery. Get you to Hillel's house, and learn the law. He speaks also in my name. What do I ask of you? Do I send you out to kill women and children? Do I ask you to go onto the holy mount and sacrifice your first-born child? NO! I ask your kindness to others, to carry out the laws remembering who gave them to you and why they were given. Of course, the written law must change with the maturing of nations. But it cannot be that each person can make the law unto his or herself. There is order in my creation, and there must be order in whatever humans shall create, including the interpretation of my law. I have given you free will. Do as you desire, but beware. You who make laws for your benefit only do it to make the life of the other harder, so that you may live in comfort. Those who deny my law of equity and take away that which belongs to others as an inheritance, and those do not adhere to the Jubilee, to those who transgress these laws will come punishment—to them and to their children. For greed and envy and hatred are passed on from parent to child, and that child, born innocent and without transgression or sin, grows to learn from the parents. Beware, lest the punishment be dire. Your creator, Ayl Elyon, did not put any human in a position to control anyone else, or to control what to do. My laws are clear. Do not quote one sentence without being sure that there is not another sentence which says the opposite of the first. If so, you must find mediation between the two. Do not pluck words and verses from the teachings in order to pervert my law. Beware of false prophets and those who tell you how to behave as a follower of righteousness. I shall be the judge of that which you do. I care not for your offerings and prayers if you then plunder the poor, forget the sick, and leave the widow and the orphan in despair. Love thy neighbor as thyself. That is the basis of the law. All else is dependent on that. I warn you, citizens of The City. If repentance is not your wont, and if adherence to your Creator's desire is not to your liking, then death and destruction shall be your reward. You shall pursue Justice in one hand, and Mercy in the other. Purchase not the judges of the land nor pervert justice, for the punishment is so great that no city has stood because of that. Remember these words, and act on them, for there is little time left for repentance. You rest on the scales of Justice and are in want. Repent and deal justly with all. If ye hearken unto my words, then Mercy shall surely rest on the scales also. Remember the words you have heard. Scribe them on scrolls, study them, and keep them in your heart, for they offer you life. Let not greed tempt you into forgetfulness."

MY DEBUT AS AN ORATOR ENDS

My mouth closed. No more words were available. The crowd remained still, and then, as if commanded by a King, quietly packed up and left the huge square. Hundreds of people were gone in a few moments, leaving me alone with three swooned, nicely dressed men, and I suppose, Ya somewhere nearby.

Then, Ya spoke once more, saying, "You did well, Mimi. I am proud of you. I just hope that at least, some of those who heard us will heed the warning, for I fear for them. But, that is the price one pays for granting free will. One can always watch but cannot make their decisions. As the great Bard will say one day, "What fools these mortals be.""

I was starving, and my stomach was grumbling its discontent, so once more I spoke, and not in a whisper. "My dear Ya. You speak of good and evil and bards to come, while my belly is empty. First feed the face, then talk Right and Wrong, for even prophets may disregard you unless they've had their customary dinners. What shall I do for sustenance? Will you rain down Manna on me, as with Moses in the wilderness? Shall I detach a stone from the wall, here, and chew it for nourishment? What would you have of me? I am both hungry and weary."

"Yes, Yes. I was about to get to that. It is not dark yet. The square is empty and will stay so till daylight. Walk beyond this platform to the other side, and you will see a tent, which shall be your lodgings for the night. The tent is next to a fountain, where you can wash and drink, for the water is pure for you. Inside the tent you will find a soft rug and your nightly meal laid out for you. Do not forget Yofi, whom you left tied in the animal pasture, outside the gate. Bring him to the fountain, so that he may also drink. He has been provided with a bin full of grasses and meal, which will delight him. Do not drink the wine to excess. You have work to do on the morrow. I bid you Shalom, and, because I am the one who is bidding it, rest assured you will not be disturbed."

I bade Ya lyla tov, although I was curious and had questions about his sleeping habits, or if he slept at all. After all, if he did sleep, and someone posed me a danger, what might happen? It was a puzzle. But I had no time for puzzles. I brought Yofi to the fountain, and we drank, and I washed, showed him to his food bin, and entered the tent. It was taller than I and was fairly large, and I could easily move about it. There was a lovely red rug on the ground and cushions strewn all around. The inside walls of the tent were decorated with the symbols of the tribes, flowers, and pretty designs. It was an extremely interesting use of design and color. A small table laden with fruits stood to one side, and all kinds of food were set out on another small table. I could see smoke rising from some of the dishes. There was a pallet off to one side piled with soft cushions, which I imagined to be my sleeping place, and I felt immensely satisfied, with the care and attention with which Ya had met my needs.

Yes, it was good. I ate, drank, made sure that Yofi was also satisfied, and then rested myself on my bed and fell asleep, wishing that Nahtahn were nearby. It is nice to be taken care of.

Daniel Aldouby

THE DAYS FOLLOWING THE PROPHECY

In the morning, the three swooners were gone, where I know not, but I surely did not miss them. I arose, saw to it that Yofi had enough to eat, washed myself and, taking Yofi with me, started walking further into the City, which was starting to stir. We had to walk down the center of the streets and alleys, because there was too much dirt and slop near the walls of the houses. Here and there, I saw the cleaners of streets doing their rounds and soon arrived at the Mount. I decided to leave Yofi tied up near a moneychanger's booth and to go up to the Temple. There were other moneychangers all around — a necessary need for travelers, because only shekels were to be used for Temple purposes, and no foreign coins could be used to buy the sacrificial animals or be used as donations. I learned this from Yoni's donkey keeper. Oh! What learning may be had from one's travels. I marveled at all I had picked up in just a short time.

As I strolled along, the aromatic smells of spices and cooking food and the sound of strange accents made we wonder at this marvelous place of gathering. There was one stall, with a table and chairs in front, and a man with a large pan filled with wood, which had been blackened and had fire burning. A grill on this pan made of long strips of black metal, of a kind I had never seen, had meat cooking right over the coals of wood. I asked the man what the black metal was, and he told me that it was the new rage, which had been introduced a while ago by the Philistines, a group which had come from an island located in the big ocean between us and Rome. He said that they made it out of rocks hewn from the soil. I could hardly believe that tale. This metal was called barzel (iron) — another amazing discovery for my remembrance! What a joy, discovering all these wonders right here in our land. I looked forward to bringing barzel bars home for cooking. I would be so proud to make Ima's work easier for her. The man cooking the meat looked at me, and, after a short eyeing, he spoke, saying, "Excuse me, but are you very busy, and are you a bit hungry?

I answered, "No and yes, Adon Mocher." Being a woman of politeness, I addressed him formally as "Mr. Seller," since we had not been introduced. He roared with laughter and said, "Well, excuse me. I am Shlomo, the Caterer — finest meats to be eaten, made with special herbs brought from faraway lands, and fit for royalty. The reason I asked you these questions is that I need help. You see, my wife is expecting to deliver our child and I here, not knowing if today shall be her time. I feel I should leave my stall and go home to see how she is. Would you mind taking my place while I leave? I do not know how long I shall be gone, but be sure that I shall return before sunset. Could you do that mitzvah?. I shall show you what must be done and how to accept payment and all the rest necessary to run this business. Only say that you will help this needy, nervous husband. B'vakasha — please?"

What could I say? I had left poor Yofi behind, to wait for me, and here was this poor man, longing to be with his wife. Choosing to help this man, I went behind the fire, and he smiled in thanks. He showed me how to be a cooker of meats in the big City and then left, to see to his family. I spent a busy afternoon selling burnt meat and wondering about what next would befall Yofi and myself. As I thought about it, I remembered Nahtahn and his promise. Oh, I wished he could be with me, now, here. But every time my thoughts went down that road, some hungry person would interrupt them. Of course, there were a few men, some coarse, who invited me to join them in pleasure, seeking things other than food, but I told them that Yofi was my friend and partner and very jealous, and that he was within calling distance. I did not further tell them about Yofi — just his name. That seemed to end those discussions.

I FINISH MY RETAILING EXPERIENCE

Finally the Mocher Basar — the meat seller, returned and told me that the attending women had told him that it would take longer to finish his wife's delivery, since it had not yet started, and they had chased him out of the house, since it was not his place to be there at that time. I thought that odd, since, if I were in pain or expecting to give birth, I would wish my dearest one to be there with me, holding my hand and comforting me. "Oh well," I thought, "That must be the way they do it in the City. How strange."

He thanked me over and over and handed me a bag full of shekels, and I could also see a gold coin or two mingling with my pay. Had I not needed the money, I would not have accepted it, since my aid was an act of help, without thought of pay. I told him so, but he insisted that I take it; otherwise, he would forever feel bad for using my services. And so, we bargained. Finally I agreed to take one-half the shekels in the bag and leave the rest for him. After all, he was to be a father and would need his earnings for his wife and descendants. Finally, he accepted this argument, and we wished each other peace and fulfillment as we parted ways.

It was mid-afternoon, and the Temple beckoned me. I walked through the handsome gate and saw, in front of me, a large courtyard and, straight ahead, the holy Parochet, the curtain in front of the Holy of Holies, where the Ark rested, and which was entered, by the High Priest, only on the one, most awe-filled day of the year, Yom Kippur. Luckily, this was not that day, and I had feasted well, as I had worked, but had it been that special day, I would have had to fast, without food or water, from sunset to sunset. There were ordinary people milling around with animals for the next sacrificial services. I knew that there were people here for transgression offerings, peace offerings of thanks, and vow offerings. I thought, to myself that this was really not something I would enjoy. I knew the story of Har Moriah, where Abraham had taken Itzhak, to sacrifice him at Ya's command, and of how Ya had stopped the sacrifice to indicate to the world that child or other human sacrifice was not according to Ya's will and was forbidden. It was at that time that Abraham instituted the animal sacrifice. But, I thought, even this was not really the way to keep Ya happy. Having met our God, I knew that he could do anything. So, if he wanted to eat meat, he could create meat already dead, and that would be a good thing for living creatures. As I thought, my head started to hurt, and so I turned to thoughts other than blood. A picture of Nahtahn's face and mop of hair appeared to me as I walked. Oh! If he were only here! As I walked out of the Temple Courtyard, going toward the moneychanger's booth, a voice whispered in my ear, "Mark this route well, Mimi, for you shall retrace your steps before you leave my City. Now, as you release Yofi, hold the rope lightly, and he shall lead you to your next meeting."

"And pray tell, oh Mighty Ya, why is it that a donkey shall be my guide? And what of this meeting you mention? Exactly what am I to expect, and who is it I am to meet; how long shall this meeting be, and what will we talk about?"

"Mimi, Mimi. You ask too many questions. You show many doubts. You must learn to trust your creator, for have I not seen that you are protected from harm, fed, and kept satisfied? Do you really wish me to tell you of all that you will learn, and all that you will experience, and all that you will become? If I do so, the rest of your long existence would be such a boring procession of years, you would always regret this impetuous demand which you make. For now, do that which I command, and we shall discuss what happens at a later time. Now, go get Yofi, and do as I have said. It will darken soon, and I do not wish you to be walking dark streets at night. Hurry, now."

I DO NOT GET A TEACHER

When I got back to the moneychanger's stall, I gave him my thanks and a few shekels as a rental fee for Yofi's space and straw, and taking Yofi by his rein, I wished my new friend a healthy and long life and walked along side Yofi's ear, so that he could listen to my whisper.

"Yofi, we have to go to a meeting. Ya says that you should take me there. You go, and I will follow you here, right behind your ear, and I'll softly sing to you while we go." He nodded and started walking, with me at his side, and I sang David's shepherd song to him, followed by the Where Does My Help Come From, followed by Yofi's favorite Hallelujah song. Oh, we had such a good time finishing the day. Finally, after many twists and turns, we came to a wall, with a gate, where Yofi stopped, pointed his nose, and gave a short bray. I tried to open the door, but it was locked. I knocked. It was answered by a stocky man, with broad shoulders. "And what is it that you wish to sell?" he asked.

"Nothing," I replied, "I have been sent here by Ayl Elyon, for a meeting. May I enter?"

"What?" shouted the man. "You dare to blaspheme, woman? You dare to invoke the Creator's name to gain entrance to see that sage of the Sanhedrin, the Great Rav Shammai?. Begone, wench! The likes of you are not welcome here!" And with that, he slammed and locked the door.

Amazed at my "welcome," I looked at Yofi, and Yofi returned my gaze. He slowly turned and continued walking down the street. After a few minutes, he stopped once more, and his nose was pointed at a doorway. I pushed at the door, and it opened. I put my head in, looked around at a pretty garden, but saw no one. I called out, "Shaloo-oom! Is there anyone home?"

I heard the sound of a door opening, and a little old man came hobbling slowly toward me.

"Well, do not stand there just looking. Come in. Take your donkey to the back, where he will find water in the pond and fresh-cut grass to eat. You do not have to tie him up, because you can close the gate to the back fence and he can safely graze and be content. Then join me in the house. The front door will be open for you." He turned and went back into the house.

I did as he had said, and Yofi made himself very comfortable. I told him that I would be in the house, and that if he needed me for anything, to utter a brayer. He did not appreciate my joke, and gave me an ear nip in rebuke. I made up with him by stroking him and telling him that I adored him and was glad that he was my traveling companion. Mollified, he drank and started grazing. I left to go into the house.

I FINALLY GET A TEACHER

Upon entering, I admired the furnishing of the home. The walls were covered with wool mats, which had pretty floral designs in bright colors. In another room, the designs were more subdued, with patterns of squares, circles, and lines the only decorations. In this room there was a table with four benches, which could seat many people. My host and I were the only ones in the room.

"Come, come, Mimi, be seated. We have so little time, and you have so much to learn. We must get started, now."

I was absolutely amazed. He knew my new name. He knew me. Who was this person? Why was I here for this meeting? Ya had dealt with me in mysterious ways before, but this was the most perplexing.

"All right," I said. "Perhaps, since you know who I am, you might introduce yourself, so that I shall know how to address you, adoni."

"Certainly," he replied. "My Name is Hillel, and I am a Rav, the head of an academy, and a leader of the Sanhedrin. You have been sent here for an intensive short course in current events and what your reply to these events may be. You will have to pay close attention, for your time with me is limited, and the learning must be much. As for how I know about you — that puzzles also me. You see, two nights ago, I dreamt that I should have a charming visitor to whom I must teach all of my accumulated wisdom in a very short time. When I awoke, I realized, having remembered every detail of the dream, that this must be a message from the one and only, praised be, our Creator. So

I sat here and waited for you. Now you tell me how you got here."

It seemed to me that Ya might have prepared Rav Hillel for me, but I was uncertain how to tell my story. Should I tell it all in detail? What should I tell, and what should I not tell? I was puzzled. Hillel looked at me for a moment and then said,
"Look. I shall get something for us to eat and drink. While I do that, look inside yourself and then decide how to proceed. I leave you to your thoughts." And he left.

I mulled my options. And then, of course, that still small voice came barging into my head. "Look, Mimi, tell him that you had a vision and that, in that vision, you were told to find him, that you might learn from him, so that you could help people to be righteous. That should be a sufficient explanation. Do not get all bound up with the details. Remember, you have a meeting in less than six weeks, and you would not wish to keep a young man waiting, would you?"

"Oh, no, my dear Ya. I will waste no time while I am with Rav Hillel. But, tell me, is Nahtahn well? Does he miss me? Oh, tell me."

"Really, Mimi. All I can tell you is that he is not unwell and that he has not forgotten the appointment which he made with you. But as for his feelings, well — you should know better than to ask me to describe what is in his heart. I leave that for him to do. Don't you think it is better that way?"

"No, I don't" said I. "I know that you know what he knows, and you do not want me to know what he knows, and I really want to know. How am I to live for more than five weeks, knowing that you know and that you will not tell me? Do you not think that is a cruel thing to do? Is the Creator of all a cruel master? Does the God of all not pity his servant who is greatly in travail? Please, please."

A crack of thunder ripped the outdoors, and the house shook. And the still, small voice whispered,

"I am the kindest you shall ever experience. Remember, I created kindness. No, I will not answer you because I must leave it to Nahtahn to speak for himself. He is a free person, and I cannot speak for him, just as I cannot act for him. Don't you remember when we discussed free will? I gave this to all humans, and I also gave them the Yetzer Harah — the inclination and choice to do evil. I do not interfere with those principles. Everyone born of woman faces those choices on a daily basis. Be an attentive learner. You should enjoy this teacher." And Ya was gone.

I LIVE AND LEARN

For a whole month, I lived in that home. My bedroom was in a corner of the rear of the house, so that I could see the back yard and the side yard. Sometimes, before going to bed, I would sit by the small window and talk and sing to Yofi, who, being joined by some geese, a cow or two, and some cats, seemed to be enjoying himself with his newfound friends. It also appeared that he had told them of my singing prowess, and they all joined in sitting under my window as I sang to them. But, for those four weeks, the hours of most of the daylight were taken up with discussions between Rav Hillel and myself. Mostly it was the Rabbi who talked, for what he had to say was the most fascinating conversation I had ever had. He discussed the five books of Moses as if he had written them. He talked of the prophets and writings as if he had been present in their time and place. And yet, his interest in all the various little details and events was not as important as the conclusions he came to after studying. He could take the most obscure verse and not only make sense of it but could make a person see a need for its necessary inclusion in the context of the writing and the importance of its place in time. He told me that his study of the Greek philosophers had allowed him to modify his thinking about interpretation of the law. For one thing, he astounded me one day by telling me the story of a pagan who had come to him with a challenge — that Hillel should teach him the entire Law while standing on one foot! If he could do that, then the pagan would convert to Hillel's religion. Have you ever heard such nonsense? Yet this pagan DID convert when Hillel stood on one foot and said, "That which is hateful unto you, do not do to any other person. That is the Law. All else is commentary."

Wasn't that brilliant? What a marvelous man was this teacher of mine. He taught me to think and analyze, criticize, and rethink until my head seemed to be a beehive swarming with new ideas, ways of thinking, and an appreciation of Ya's achievement in giving us such a fine brain, which could encompass so many wonderful things, along with different ways of thinking, with which we could test our thoughts and experiences. The more I stayed with Hillel, the more I looked upon him as my mind's father. I praise Ya for this blessing I received, especially after the rudeness I had experienced at Rav Shammai's home. But, then again, who am I to judge people's character? So, I shall not judge Shammai, except to say that I was treated rudely and surely not the in manner our ancestor Abraham would have treated me. Maybe it is that Shammai still had studying to do in order to learn how a human should behave. Oh well. I shall forget about petty hurts and always remember my dear teacher, the Elder Hillel.

LABORS IN THE FIELDS BEGIN

At the end of the four-week period, just after the New Moon, Rav Hillel and I bade each other farewell, with many tears of mine like raindrops on his floor. He told me that I had been a fine and willing student and, not knowing what lay in store for me, told me to be strong in my knowing and unafraid of truth, He warned me that there were many false prophets twisting the Creator's truth in pursuit of their own wealth or for power. He told me that there were priests who were venal and cared not for the law but only for personal honors and glory and even riches. He said that there were crazy people who went off by themselves to form their own congregations, unwilling to join with others and unwilling to wed and to multiply. At this point, he just shook his head and said that this was a direct profanation of the Creator's name and reputation. He said to watch out for the wealthy among the people, for they had forgotten about Ya's basic themes of justice for all, care for the sick and needy, seeing to the needs of widows and orphans, and preserving the dignity of each person in the world. He said that these people lavishly provided sacrifices and gifts to the priests but which were ill-gotten gains ripped from the widows and the poor. There were landlords who had deliberately disregarded the Jubilee Years, thus amassing lands which did not rightfully belong to them. That there were people in the city who preferred the Greek games to the study of the law. Hillel, in this regard, had several opinions.

The practice in the Gymnasium of doing athletics without clothes was, to him, utter abomination and contrary to all of our laws. But fitness of body should be practiced because the body contained our lives, and that spark, that divine image which makes us do Mitzvot. He told me that all the study in the world and all the professions of love of a Creator were nothing without doing good, which the Creator desires. I was shocked when he told me that even people who said that they did not believe in a god but who nevertheless carried out the commandments of thoughtfulness and regard for the health and wellbeing of others — those people were his creations also and that their deeds merited reward. I, at first attempted to argue, saying that pagans could not be good people, for lack of knowledge of the law. Yet, when he told me that the pagan is judged by deeds alone, while we who know of our Creator must do all these ethical and moral things precisely because of the law. It was difficult for me to accept, and I finally gave up arguing when Hillel told me I would understand it more when I matured. Huh — I was almost nineteen and was already mature. But I did not say this, for fear of getting into another argument I could not hope to win. It is difficult to argue with the kindest, wisest one ever to be encountered. But, oh, I could tell of other wondrous ideas, rules, and thoughts. But my story must continue.

I left my second home and my beloved teacher, with Yofi at the end of the rein, and we just walked and walked and walked, until we had come to the end of city and a ravine-like place, located in a valley called Gehinom and which was called Azazel. This was where the trash was heaped, far down and away from the city walls. This was where, at night, the jackals and wild animals came to feast and eat each other. It was not a nice place. In fact, within a week, I learned that the inhabitants of the City had a way of cursing their enemy with a short phrase 'Laych Lazazel!" Go to

Azazel! This meant that the people being cursed merited the trash heap as a dwelling place. Not a nice thought at all, and certainly not among civilized people. After seeing this horrible human-made heap of leavings and wild creatures, Yofi and I turned back to the inner city, for that still, small voice had come to me in the night and told me to return to the Temple Gates.

ME AND MY MOUTH

I asked the moneychanger to, once more, care for Yofi and entered the Temple courtyard. There appeared to be some sort of discussion going on in one corner. Walking over, I saw a priest and a woman arguing. The woman had a complaint. The whole of the complaint was centered around an idea that it was only the sons of Aaron who were to be priests, and, from the time of Solomon's Temple, until the time of the overthrow of the Syrian Pagans, all the High Priests had been descended from Zadok. Now, it seems that the High Priests had been descended from Matityahu and his sons. And lately, there has been some doubt whether the High Priest can claim descent from any one of note. She said that there had been rumors that the priesthood could be bought. She demanded to know, before she brought any more sacrifices, what, exactly, was going on. She said she was not going to bring any offerings until the matter was settled. The priest called her a pagan, and worse, and tried to push her toward the gate. I stood there, horrified. Is this the way holy priests act? Is this the way civilized men act? This was not how I pictured our Temple to be.

Suddenly, a great anger arose within me, and my body rushed to the woman's side. I placed myself between the two of them and faced him. Without thinking, my mouth opened itself and the words flowed like a mountain stream in the rainy season.

"You who call yourself a holy priest. You, the self-proclaimed servant of Temple Worship. Now hear the words of your Melech, Ayl Shaddai! Have I ever commanded that the priests should lay their hands on my people in anger? These hands, which bless and praise, cannot be against my people. Thou hast transgressed against this woman, as thou hast transgressed by bribing, by taking bribes, by accepting less-than-perfect offerings, by immersing the Temple in affairs best left to the elders of the city. You have only one of two choices, miscreant. Because of these transgressions, thou art banished from the Temple Grounds. Within these walls thou shalt no longer be seen. Should you transgress in this, thou shalt surely die. Now leave! The Lord has spoken."

And a bolt of lightning streaked across the sky over the Holy of Holies. There was silence, and the priest rushed into the Temple building and disappeared. The woman looked at me and, in a very serious, quiet voice asked, "Who are you, that you speak so confidently to a holy man?"

I thought for a moment before speaking.

"Holiness is not a permanent condition. It is the doing and the intention behind the doing which may confer holiness. This man gave up any pretension to his status with his uncivil behavior. No one has the right to push a woman around. Not even the High Priest. It is forbidden. I do know that, in the Torah, it speaks briefly of a husband hitting his wife, but that was before we had sages who could interpret the meaning of that section. A restriction was placed on this beating — that the instrument used should be a stick of a certain, small length, no larger than a thumb. Now think! In a moment of temper, which men have overmuch, a husband may wish to strike his wife. He must then search for the beating stick. If he can't find it, then he must go out, find another stick, and ensure that it meets the requirements. Any man, in general being flighty of mind, would easily forget anger and thus be reconciled once more to his wife. In this way, the Yetzer Harah is subdued, and no harm can follow. I would tell you that, if a man does beat his wife, then the wife has the right not only to beat him back but to do so in such a way that he never repeats that despicable behavior. There should be respect, before and after a marriage takes place, for all people who feel the emotion of love. In respect and love, we find the beginning of holiness. This is the meaning of what has happened here today."

The people around us stood silent, gaping and staring. I did not understand at that time why, but I later found that this was the first time that someone such as I had dared to speak thusly to a
priest; furthermore, never before had a woman stood in this place, in Jerusalem, as I had, and prophesied in Ya's name. They did not know what to make of this. Suddenly, there was a tumult, and a group of men rushed from the interior, armed with knives and blades. They did not look anything like holy priests, for they were wide-eyed and screaming, as they headed straight for me. I stood still, and, trusting in Ya, I pointed at them and said,

"Sleep, children of evil inclinations, until the sun rises once more, and when you arise, you shall go home and harm no one as long as you live."

As I said the first word — "Sleep" — the men halted as if they had hit a wall. They did not move until I had finished speaking, and then they dropped to the ground in a deep sleep. At this happening, the priest whom Ya had banished walked out, ashen-faced, and with head bowed low. He exited through the Temple Gates, a pitiful sight, completely changed from the proud, vain, pompous person he had been just a short time before.

THE NEXT WEEK COMES

The woman I had defended asked me if I would honor her by coming home with her for a meal. I accepted, and we went to collect Yofi. As we wended our way to her home, she explained to me that the men who had rushed to attack me were known as Sicaari and were religious fanatics who believed in the letter of the law without any explanation or interpretation. She shocked me with the tales of how, when armies had come to capture Jerusalem, these Sicaari, on the Shabbat, would go up on the city walls, and stab and kill the brave men defending the city, because those idiots thought that the fighters should not be doing their work on the day of rest. I thought this the strangest thing I had ever heard and realized that there were people amongst us who had gone mad over their beliefs and had transgressed beyond the will of Ayl; even the Day of Atonement held no hope for them. There could never be a good relationship between them and their Creator. Oh, how I wished that men would not act so stupidly. It pained me that their parents had not taught them how to be a good person.

In her home, Rivka, for that was her name, offered me a bowl of hot lentil soup, with bread she, herself, had baked, followed by a lamb stew, which was welcomed by my mouth and nose for its taste and smell. She introduced me to her husband, a miller named Bar-Eber, for he had been born on the other side of the river. He was a pleasant-enough man, and we all chatted about the day's events. He was pleased with his wife, for they had had many discussions about the Temple scandals. He laughed when I told him how his wife had berated the priest, and he remarked. "Better the priest than me. I know my beloved's temper and would not wish to disturb it." And he gave her such a loving glance that it reminded me of my loneliness and the absence of Nahtahn.

"Oh, time, rush quickly forward and use up the days, so that my heart once more will be nourished." That thought reminded me that, six days hence, my loneliness would end, and I once more was able to smile.

Rivka showed me the extra room, where her daughter — who was now married — had slept as a child, and offered it to me. Yofi was comfortable in the back of the house, where Bar-Eber's donkey also was kept. So I accepted the gracious offer and slept.

RIVKA IS SURPRISED AGAIN

After the day we had lived through, I slept very well, and, in the morning, my hosts and I exchanged a Boker Tov, and everyone was in a cheerful mood. Rivka and I cleaned up quickly and fed the animals, and we had to go shopping for the day's supply of food. You know, of course, that refrigerators were unknown in those days, so shopping at the food market was a daily chore. I went to tell Yofi that I would not be with him for a short while but that I would return soon. He looked at me mournfully, ears drooping. We both took along a straw basket and walked the short distance to the market, where we bought vegetables and flour for baking and spent some time looking at fabrics, furniture, rugs, and other household things of interest. One thing which surprised me was a large shop filled with all sizes of statues. Rivka told me not to look, because the owner was a pagan who sold idols. I found out that his business was doing well, because there were many people who practiced all kinds of beliefs, and who came from other lands, and that there were even some descendants of Abraham who did the same as the foreigners. I was shocked and horrified. This was the first time that I had come into the company of people who did not worship the Giver of the Law. We turned to go back and had gone but a short way when we were accosted by some men and women who recognized us from the day before.

"Hah! So, the two Queens of the Temple go shopping. The blasphemers and slanderers walk abroad, bold-faced and unashamed!" shouted one of them.

Another sneered, "Yes, show us your magic, perchance a sleeping potion, or other trick. How dare you show your faces after you despoiled the air in the Temple Courtyard? You are probably witches and do not deserve to live here with…"

Before he could say another word, the skies, which had been blue, darkened. The sun was gone, and only a dim light shone down from the heavens, completely encircling the angry man. A fierce wind blew around him, disturbing the dirt and dust at his feet. The wind blew louder and faster, and, then, he was twirling, caught in that circle of noise, until he just disappeared. The noise stopped. The darkness became daylight. As we looked around to see what had happened, it was as it was before, except that the man who had spoken to us so rudely had vanished. His companions looked around, looked up, peered at us, and turned to flee, but, as they ran, they kept tripping and falling, tripping and falling. It was a sight to behold.

Rivka and I marveled at what had happened. Then we finished our shopping and left the market. Rivka looked at me and spoke slowly. "I have lived a goodly number of years, Mimi, and never have I heard of what I have witnessed these past two days. I know that you are here to fulfill a mission vow, but what of these miraculous things — men dropping as if dead and enemies just disappearing in a wind. How do you do it?"

"I really do not know, Rivka. Just as Moses had nothing to do with the making of the plagues but acted only as a messenger, so it is with me. When I am commanded at times to open my mouth, I do so, and my voice comes by itself, the words gushing out, with no planning on my part.

Our creator works in ways unknown to us, but we know of the accomplishments. The voice which I hear is neither man's nor woman's but a little of both. I would imagine that, although we are created in the Creator's image, and that since both men and women are created in that image, then either our Creator must be one of two beings: A combination of both, or one which is neither. This is too large a thing for me to understand, so I just accept the fact that the Creator exists. Otherwise, I may be mad and have left my mind somewhere in the Kinneret, with my washing. I don't know. I just don't know."

"You know, Mimi, I think I can just begin to see what you are saying, but it is too difficult for me to understand it all, too. Well, maybe that is all to the good, also. If I spent my time worrying about that, Bar-Eber would have to cook his own dinner, which is why, now that we have arrived home, I must get busy."

And so, we got to work washing and cutting vegetables, and cooking. There is a time to think, and there is a time to do. I went out to the back, greeted Yofi and his friends, and sang the song of how the mountains danced, and how they pranced like sheep before the Almighty God of Jacob. Oh, how they loved it! The donkeys brayed along, and the goats pranced and jumped. It was a good time for all.

Then Eber came home, and we sat down for the evening meal. Before we ate, Eber picked up a piece of bread and held it, saying, "Just think. A very long time ago, when our people did not farm, they were wandering with their flocks. Every Springtime, they would see the earth spring forth with new growth for their flocks and were amazed by this yearly miracle. Now, of course, in these modern times, we know that each plant has its seeds, which are dropped on the ground, ready for the next rains. Our Lord has surely created a perfect world, which is good. My father used to praise this creation before each meal. Here is what he said: 'Praised be Ayl, our God, Creator of the world, who causes bread to spring from the earth.' We now know that this is not an accident but that it was planned from the beginning. Is it not extraordinary how this seemingly varied plant and animal world is really understandable and orderly? We have come a long way since our shepherd days in the wilderness.

I wondered how far we had really come when I thought of the mean people I had met in my travels. But then, I changed my mind. In the scales of my experience, there had been more good done for me than evil. Strangers had taken me in, fed me, sheltered me, and helped me learn.

We ate and conversed, and, after cleaning up, we went to our sleeping chambers. I knew that tomorrow would be my last day here. It would be full moon, and, the morning after, I would be reunited with Nahtahn. I thought of that beautiful name, and it came to me that the name itself meant "given," like a gift. Oh, could this also be a sign? How I longed for the hours to pass. And then, I fell asleep. I dreamt I was with Ima and telling her about Nahtahn — how beautiful and polite he was. She was telling me to be patient and not to expect too much, lest I be disappointed later on. She added that a young woman, who thinks she is in love with a man, may be in love only with an idea, a dream of love. But, she did not advise me to avoid meeting him. I suddenly awoke from that dream and thought it strange that I should dream of Ima this night, when I had not dreamt of her since leaving home. Then, once more, I slept.

THE LAST DAY OF MY WAIT

In the morning, having nothing else to do, I ate hurriedly, went out to see to Yofi, and, knowing that Rivka had set out earlier to visit her mother, I decided to wander through the city and see more of it before I left. Walking at a leisurely pace made it easier to study the people and activity on the streets. My footsteps took me through alleys or streets with small vendor stalls, great and small homes, and people — lots of people, hurrying here and there. No one was strolling leisurely. I wondered what their hurry was all about. So, I stopped a few of them and asked, "Slicha. Why are you hurrying? Is there someone hurt? Is there a fire? Can I help?"

Most of the people did not even bother to answer. Some of them said something like, "I am going to the shuk, to buy something" or "I have go see someone " or "I am hurrying home." Only one person stopped to converse.

She said, "Why do you ask?"

"Because I come from a small place on the shores of Kinneret, and when we walk, our pace is much slower so that we can see the beauty of the trees, flowers, and sky, and, if we see something interesting such as a beautiful flower or an animal, we stop and look. I do not see people doing that here. I was wondering why, because, although the scenery may be different, nevertheless, there are many interesting sights and goings on, and, if one does not hurry, one might notice a friend in passing or even stop and make a new friend. This rushing around seems very curious to me."

"Ah," said the woman. "You do not know city life well. Look around you. Do you see many empty spaces? Do you see open fields? You see houses almost leaning on each other, as if to take a little more space. You see narrow streets. You see many people. There is very little space for privacy, so in order to live close together like this, people try to respect whatever space which others have for privacy. Of course, when friends happen upon each other, they greet and exchange family news, but in general, city folks use the streets only as a way of getting somewhere else without tarrying. If they wish to have a leisurely walk, they will go outside the city walls and find a pretty spot. Those places are few, and so poor people really have no greenery and strolling places, except for the backs of homes, where animals are kept, if they have back yards and animals. Those who have wealth can close their homes and take their families north to places where there is natural beauty, or down to the Salt Sea, for a warm salt swim to invigorate the skin. There are also bathing oases here and there but, again, only for those who can afford to travel. Now, does that answer your question, my dear? I hope it does, for I am on my way to the shuk. We need a new cooking pot, and I cannot decide whether to get earthenware or metal. My husband grumbles that he does not like to eat what is cooked in dirt, and I feel that metal might be harmful if it gets into the food. I shall have to ask the merchants and other women of their thoughts."

I thanked her very much for all the valuable information I had taken in from her and wished her a full and peaceful life as we parted ways. I liked her. Why is it that the women were so welcoming to my questions and the men so angry? It was a puzzlement.

I CONFRONT DISSENSION

I continued my wandering, and, walking through a small neighborhood square, I heard shouting and argument. There was a group of men all talking and gesturing, and no one seemed to be listening. Drawing near, I heard the names "Shammai" and "Hillel" being shouted. I paid attention for a long while, and I began to understand what was happening. There seemed to be two points of view being argued. It appeared that those who were adherents of Shammai were arguing for a strict adherence to the letter of the Law, with no exceptions. They reasoned that, since the Law came from God, it was immutable and could not be changed by man. The Hillel followers were arguing that, since the law was a gift to us, it was up to us to determine how it was to be used and what the gift meant. The argument raged back and forth, until the gesturing became very threatening, and I feared that people would get hurt.

As the heat started to rise among these men, I suddenly felt light-headed and was afraid I would swoon on the spot, so I leaned against a wall on one side of the square and took deep breaths. Suddenly, I knew that Ya was in action, for, out of the blue sky came a bolt of lightning which, thankfully, hit no one. Then as I expected, from my past experience, I felt my mouth open, and knew what was about to happen — and it did. The words came tumbling out of my mouth, and there I was, talking to these men of ill temper.

"Thus speaks Hashem (the Name), your Creator. What mean you by invoking the names of your teachers to preach your opinion? Have I not taught you that, when two opposing statements appear to contradict each other, you must find a third statement which reconciles them? You threaten each other without using the brains you were born with. Hear my words, and follow closely. Yes, my laws are immutable. Yes I have given them to you. Yes, you must read these laws as they pertain to time, person, and place. The law for the shepherd of Abraham's time was not the same as the law for Aaron's time. The laws for a shepherding people cannot be the same as for farmers. In the case of farmers, there is the necessity for personal real property rights. This cannot be the case for the wandering shepherds and the flocks, for it depends on the place and the season, where they will be. The law cannot be the same for the infant and for the older people. We must allow for interpretation so that the law makes sense and may be followed. Shammai declares the authority of the law. Hillel declares how it shall be used for the good of all. Now! Go you, each one, to your homes and ponder this. To discuss questions of the law is good, but fighting over extremes and not finding solutions is a waste of life. Remember these words, for I will not be satisfied until all of you understand the intent of the Law — not to punish, but to help humans grow into righteousness. Shammai is correct — The Law is the Law. Hillel is correct — all the laws are commentaries on how you relate to each other and to your Maker. GO!" And with that, came another clap of thunder, and, startled, the men ran off in different directions. I alone was left.

"Well done, Ya," I said, "No one had to swoon, and no one had to disappear. It was the Word which impressed them. I, too, was impressed, because I dismissed Shammai as a boor, and I can see now that he is the chair to Hillel's table. Yes, I am proud of you."

"Proud of ME? Of Me, your creator, your voice? Aren't we a bit bigger with our mouth than is proper for a lady in Jerusalem? Where are your manners? I have no need for your pride or for your compliments, for I am the Lord. But I can understand your eagerness and your impression of my prowess. Yet, understand this: No matter how powerful I may be, the mind of humans is not mine to control. It is each individual who is responsible for the decisions of the mind and the possible outcomes. Now, go back, pack up, and prepare for a long trip. You have an appointment tomorrow, just after sunrise. You must be ready. I assure you, you will have a restful sleep. Go."

And so, I left.

NIGHT AND ANTICIPATION

When I arrived at Rivka and Eber's home, I was greeted by loud brays, cacklings, bleatings, and honks. Rushing to the rear enclosure, I saw two roosters fighting and biting each other.
Separating them, I told them that they should settle down. and I held them apart. I came up with an idea. I tied one to a post in one corner of the yard and the other one to the opposite post. Then I addressed the flock. "Now you hens have your choice. No more fighting."

I thought I was very clever and smiled. However, I noticed that the flock was quiet and that no one was cackling to anyone else. I dismissed the silence as a kind of shock at the changed state of affairs and thought that they would get accustomed to it. I petted Yofi and went in to eat. Rivka and Eber had started to sup, and I joined them in a delicious meal of skewered lamb, with pitah. I thanked them both for their wonderful hospitality and told them that I had changed my mind about city people. I now knew that there were some good and some bad and that I should not make up my mind when I first arrived anywhere. They smiled at me and told me how much I reminded them of their daughter when she had been my age. I took that to be a great compliment. I then told them that I was leaving just before the sun could be seen and embraced them both with tears in my eyes, and we went to our rooms. I whispered out of my window my goodnight to Yofi, and, just before falling asleep, I once again had a vision of a lovely, smiling face, broad shoulders and the morrow's meeting.

A JOYOUS REUNION AND SURPRISE

At dawn, I quietly arose, went to awaken Yofi, and fed him amply with straw, grass, and water. I had some food supplies, pitah and fruit, for I had decided to purchase whatever else I required at the shuk, inside the city gates. As Yofi and I trotted toward my meeting, my heart was so full of song that I began to sing to Yofi. Yofi joined in whenever he liked what he heard. As we neared the gate court, the sun warmed our bones, and our pace hastened. After reaching the court, I stopped for a moment, purchased some more fresh fruits, pitah, and some cooked lamb, and we headed for the Great Gate. As we left, I looked around, hoping to see that face I longed for. Then, I heard my name. I looked backward, for the voice seemed to be behind us, and there was Nahtahn, smiling. Yofi and I quickly turned to retrace our steps and greet him. Nahtahn descended, as did I, and we stood with just the width of my thumb separating our noses. We just stared and stared and stared at each other. No words came to my mouth. I felt like flinging myself at him and enwrapping him with my being yet feared to be so bold. I had never experienced such a strange urge. I would have to think on this — but later. For now I must be here and speak. But before I could ever say something like, "Peace be with you. How have you been?" Nahtahn spoke.

"And how has Mimi fared in her mission? Has the Vow been kept? I understand that you have created quite a stir by shocking many city natives out of their caftans. I also have noted that your voice changes with your moods. Tell me. Does the Creator really tell you what to say? Are you a messenger from on high? I must know, for, if you are, then I have no hope. My heart yearns to be with you, but if you are forbidden to me, I must suffer my feelings in silence and accept my fate. Please, oh please — explain."

"Oh Nahtahn, I cannot give you a full answer to all your questions, but first, let us find a quiet spot outside the gates where we will be away from the noise, and then we shall talk."

And so, in a little while, we came to a stream and rested under a tree while Yofi and Hamor grazed on the grass. Then I remembered all that Nahtahn had said and blurted out, "How did you know what has happened to me the past five or six weeks? You were far south of here and could not have known of my experiences and the events of my life. How do you know?"

"My dear Mimi, do you think that I would leave you here, in the big city, knowing no one? Did you think I would desert my new dear friend? I could not do so. I had traveled just a short way, enough to let you enter, and then retraced my steps and followed you to ensure your safety, for I knew that you were innocent of the ways of the city. I did not want to interfere with your stated mission, and so I hid myself from your view at all times. But be assured, I was there. How could I not be there? Had something happened to you, I would have lived with regret and pain. No! I felt it my responsibility to look after you. That is how I know of your stay."

I was aware that he did not know of the presence of Ya and that I was very safe at all times. But I did not know how to respond and needed time before speaking. So, I arose, saying, "I must go for a short walk and think on this surprise. If you will wait here, I shall return, and we will talk further."

He gave a start but made no move to stop me, nor did he utter a word. He just sat there, with a forlorn look and as I looked at him, my soul urged me to rush to him and encircle him in my arms. I, however, thought it better to seek help.

Walking off a little way, I whispered, in a beseeching tone, "Help me, Ya. I need advice and some sort of permission. I yearn after this man. I believe he feels the same of me. He knows not of your speaking to me, or of my mission. What should I tell him? What is forbidden for him to know of me? May I tell him of my feelings? Oh, please. I cannot bear this chasm which separates us. Tell me. What may I do? What shall I do?"

Again, as before, came that still, small voice, but this time, laden with kindness and loving, and spoke to me.

"My dear Mimi. Nahtahn is a righteous man. He knows that to be a good person, one must, sometimes, forego one's plans in order to care for others. He is kind. I would not wish for you to be alone for the rest of your life, for you are human and have your own needs, desires, and hopes. I make this pact with you. If both of you wish to be together, have a family, and grow old together, you have my blessings. You may tell him everything that has befallen you in your life. Tell him everything concerning that which you, yourself, know of your mission, but you must make him vow never to speak of it to anyone else without permission — ever. Is that understood?"

My eyes filled with tears of gladness, and my heart leapt as a young gazelle. I nodded vigorously as I spoke. "Oh, yes, Ya, dear Ya, kind Ya. I hear, and I shall obey. We have a pact, you and I. Now, if you will excuse me, I shall return to the tree and have a long talk with Nahtahn. Is that all right with you?"

"Tsk. Tsk. And just where do you think you shall go after this long talk, Mimi? I would suggest you tarry a bit, and I shall tell you when and where. Is that understood?"
I had started walking away, and, now, I had to stop and wait.
"I thought that, with the pact concluded, our conversation would be over, Ya. What is it now? Surely you do not have immediate work for me. That would be a great unkindness — do you not think so?"

"Think so? Think so? Do you really believe that the Creator who sees all, knows all, and is everywhere, has to think? I see that you still do not understand me very well. I shall overlook your question and tell you this. You and Nahtahn, having my blessing, may have one month to be alone together with each other wherever you go, inseparable. Cleave to each other, and let your love grow strong, for each of you will need that strength for years and years to come. At the end of four weeks, you will appear in Ashdod, by the great sea, and I shall instruct you further. Do not forget. Again, my blessings on the both of you and, and may your happiness be great. Now, begone."

Again uttering my thanks, I turned and left the Presence to return to my beloved.

OH DELIGHTFUL EXISTENCE

I walked back to Nahtahn, who was sitting on the ground with his head in his hands and his elbows on his knees, deep in thought. As I approached, he gave me an enquiring look, and I sat down beside him.

"Look," I said, "We met as if by accident. We traveled together and were happy not to be lonely travelers. We seemed to be very satisfied to be with each other. I have a proposal to make to you. If you wish someone who will be at your side when you need her, and if you shall do the same for me, I see no reason why we should not travel through life together. What say you?"

His head snapped up. Tears appeared in his eyes. He started to say something but stopped. Then, he took my hand looked into my eyes so deeply that I felt he knew my heart and soul — and then he spoke.

"Dear, sweet Mimi. From the moment we met, I knew that I could not be content with the rest of my life if you were not a part of it. So, knowing that you feel the same for me, I tell you that I shall never forsake you. I shall be yours, and you shall be mine. Our lives shall be one. I also must say to you that I have never met a woman as beautiful and as bright as you. I am the luckiest man who ever lived. Praised be the Creator of all, who has brought you to me."

The words tingled my ears. My heart burst with joy, and, as if we knew each other's thoughts, we took one step and embraced each other with a kiss. My eyes closed, yet I saw a firmament bright with stars, and I must say that my whole body felt a joy it had never felt before. This was very exciting, and I liked it. And I heard Nahtahn gasp.

"Look," there, way down the road — a rainbow — and all around is sunshine. How can it be?"

"Oh", I replied. "It is our God's way of blessing our marriage. You see, I received permission for us to marry."

"WHAT! Just what does that mean, Mimi? How, what, when? What is happening?"

"Come, sit down, my handsome husband, and I shall relate to you what you have married. I am sure that you will be even more surprised by events, as I describe my life to you ere we met. Come sit by my side."

As we sat by the water, I told him of my first meeting with Ya and of the other conversations which our God had had with me. I also told him that the voice he heard as I addressed crowds of people was not mine. I told him of learning with Rav Hillel and of the other people I had met. When I had ended my strange story, Nahtahn took my hands in his.

"Never have I heard a stranger tale. But I know you to be truthful, and my eyes have seen wonders around you; I have heard that voice from your lips and known that it was not yours. Truly, you must be blessed among all maidens, to be so honored. Likewise, am I fortunate and doubly blessed to be so close to one who converses with Ayl. I am humbled, for I do not know what will be my role in this

High Mission of yours. But whatever befalls us, know that I love you and deem myself to be indeed the most fortunate of all men." With that, we sealed the love in both our hearts.

MY HUSBAND AND I TRAVEL

As we headed west, toward Ashdod — for I had told my love where I had been commanded to go — we passed through a village where there resided a tentmaker. We stopped and purchased a large tent, with an additional small tent sewn on to the north side. This was for our two donkeys, as we knew the rainy season would come. And so we continued westward, stopping nightly, and enjoying our temporary home. I knew a little of the way of man and woman, for my mother had advised me at the time of my becoming a woman, and I had also seen animals making babies, so I felt quite learned in these matters. However, as the nights passed by, I learned more and more how to enjoy my body. I looked forward to the end of each day's journey.

We finally reached Ashdod, after traveling for two weeks, having traveled slowly, to prolong our moments alone, and found a strange assortment of people. There were all kinds of people, in all shades of color, and speaking not Hebrew but Aramaic, which we could also speak, for we had learned both languages as children. There were people of the sea, who lived on ships, and went from port to port engaged in trading. There were merchants who bought and sold all manner of foods and household needs. There were even different places and means of worshipping gods, some of them we had never heard of before. There were wine sellers offering their drinks early in the morning, and, by noon of the sun, many men — and also, to my surprise, women — appeared in the streets, and they were not in control of their bodies. They traveled a snake path, and one had to be careful when passing them, lest one bump into them and knock them down. We even saw some so full of wine that they just sank to the ground and slept —and this, in the morning hours. We were amazed.

We left the city, and, as evening came, we found a quiet grassy spot, not far from the sea, and pitched our tent. Then we saw there was no one else present, so we went bathing in the Yam. It was so refreshing to feel the water, and then a wave hit my face, and my eyes hurt. I did not weep but went to the sand and wiped my face. But I could taste salt, and I realized that this was the reason my eyes seemed to be burning. I was not used to this kind of swimming, because our Kinneret was lovely, sweet, fresh water, with no salt, unlike this sea. It only took a little while for the pain to go away, and, by the time Nahtahn joined me, I was feeling much better. We ate and, being tired, went to sleep.

STRANGE STRANGERS, STRANGE WAYS

Just after sunrise, as we awoke, we heard loud voices outside our tent. I looked out, and there were eight or nine men of all ages gathered around the tent, and, when they saw me, they started to shout, and what they were saying was not very polite. They said that they would like to enter the tent and play with me. They told me that I looked as if I needed them. When Nahtahn appeared at the tent opening, they shouted at him and told him that, if he valued his skin, he should leave the spot quickly. He reached next to the inside flap of the tent and drew out a gleaming sword as long as my arm. I grew frightened. I did not want a fight, and I did not want Nahtahn to be harmed. Then Nahtahn spoke.

"Gentlemen, my sword is keen. Yet I hesitate to use it, for fear of creating families without husbands or fathers. Do not force me to do that."

The largest of the men stepped forward. "Listen, boy. We told you to leave once; that is enough warning for any sensible person. It appears you have no sense. We are nine, and you are one. For the last time, I tell you — leave! Leave, or you die."

Nahtahn stepped in front of me, looked at the man, and answered.

"I tell you now, that all of you are in danger, great danger, for two reasons. The first is that this woman and I are wife and husband and our vows have been blessed by the one who created you. Be warned that the same god who punished the Pharaoh, when he enslaved our ancestors, the Habiru, is the guardian of this woman and her protector. You may be able to kill me, but should you approach her to do her harm, your punishment will be severe. Trust me."

"Ha!" said the stranger, "Know that I do not know this god of yours and have no fear of you, for my sword and those of my friends are sharp and are looking for your heart, to pluck it, and your head, to slice it off and raise it on high. Now, enough talk. I am tired of this. Come, men, let us do what we will. Follow me!"

And, with that, he rushed at Nahtahn, tripped, and fell. In falling, he managed to put a deep gash in his left arm as he tried to hold on to his sword. The other men ran at us, and, as they reached two spear lengths from us, they stopped as if they had hit a wall. Four of them were bleeding from their noses or mouths, while three of them had hit their heads hard against nothing that could be seen. They looked startled; frightened, they turned to flee but couldn't. No matter in which direction they wished to go, they were blocked. And then I knew what was to happen.

Just as I expected, my mouth opened, and the voice thundered.

"You, who deny me. If you have not heard of me, hearken unto my voice. Even if you do not know my law, do you not know the Law of Receiving the Stranger? Is this not the custom of all the peoples of the world? I tell you this. Molest not the stranger in your midst. Trouble not the traveler. Should you not heed my warning, your punishment shall be more bitter than today. Be warned, and teach your peoples, wherever you go, the Law of Receiving the Stranger as guest. You have heard the word of the Creator of All. Now, heed Me and begone!"

With those words, suddenly the place where the men stood turned all black as night — even the air — until it seemed that a huge black box stood on the sand. Then the box flew up and up and flew over the water, far out, and then flew north, and then, nine men fell from the sky into the water screaming in terror, splashing as they hit the waves, and we could see them swimming toward the shore. I was, again, impressed by the deeds of my Guardian, and, turning to Nahtahn, I murmured, "Oh, my sweet man, I feared for you but knew that Ya would protect us."

Raising my eyes up, I said, "Once more, Ya, you have acted with spectacular deeds. I must say that seeing you in action is much more interesting and exciting than donkey or camel races. Once again, I thank you for your gracious intercession."

This time, no voice came from my mouth as an answer. Instead, the still, small voice seemed to come from all around, as it spoke.

"Nahtahn, hear my words. You have been chosen to be the mate of She Who Bears My Voice. You have shown that you are able and that you have the will power, strength, and gentleness to be a proper husband. Know, that henceforth, your name shall not be Nahtahn (Given), but shall be Nahyim (Pleasant), because you have been gracious, patient, kind, and understanding, a pleasant person to

Daniel Aldouby

know. However, your joining her as husband presents a
problem. You see, Mimi shall have many lives for as long
as I need her voice. I have therefore decided that, wherever
she goes, there will you go, also. As long as she is on earth,
there will you be, also. However, I must warn you to
beware. Her manner of speech, at times, may create a
problem for you. You may have noticed that even while
she trembles, she shows no fear. In fact, I sometimes
wonder, as she converses with me, if she does not stand in
awe of or fear me. Watch over her carefully. Nahyim. She
has a fire within her."
And then, silence. Nahyim said nothing. He smiled at me.

A BREAKFAST CHAT

At sunrise, we rose after another marvelous night and ate while we discussed yesterday's encounter. Nahyim was particularly enamored of the way Ya had solved our problem. But then, Nahyim asked me, "Mimi, one thing puzzles me about the voice. I have heard Ya speak through you several times. Sometimes it sounds very gentle, as a mother would speak to her beloved child, yet, at other times, it sounds as if a warrior were lodged in you, fierce and dangerous. Why is this? What is Ya? Is Ya he or she? How do we address our creator?"

"Oh, my darling, sweet Nam-Nam. I too, have pondered that question. I have no answer, which I can say is the truth, but here is what I think, based on what I have learned thus far. For example, you are a leather worker. You take a piece of hide and create a sandal. Are you the sandal? Is the coppersmith a cup? Is the tentmaker a tent? You see where my thoughts lie. Since the Creator of all has created us, both man and woman, it might follow that the Creator cannot be as either of us. We are created in the image as a shadow is created, and so, it may be that the Creator may have thought it best to create he and she in all animals so that we could reproduce ourselves without having the knowledge to create from nothing, as did the Creator. Beside all of that, do you not think that the Creator has made it so pleasant for us in this matter?"

"Weighty thoughts, my sweet. As I think on them, I would agree with what you said, especially the pleasantness part. It is a pleasure to speak with you and listen to your explanation. Yes. I remember from the teachings how Ya created us both in the same image, yet we are different, and

I agree with you that the difference is most pleasant for me also. Oh, how blessed we are. Yet, what now? What are we to do? Where do we go?"

"I do not know, beautiful man. When the time comes for us to go or do, we shall know of it. For now, let us lie outside and bask in the warmth of the day. We do not know when we shall have to leave this lovely nest. Come, I shall spread a covering on the sand."

So the rest of the day was spent, sitting, lying, swimming, and holding each other close. Seldom have such days been in my life. Silently, I thanked Ya for my being, my body, my feelings, and for my husband, who had treated them all so well. The days went by thusly, and I wished that this delightful way of living would go on forever; however, it was not to be. Within four days, as we basked in the setting sun, that voice returned saying,

"Listen, both of you. Tomorrow, you are to go to the market square in Ashdod, where you will address the crowd, and I, of course, shall be with you. Be there at mid-morning."

That was all. We bowed our heads in understanding. We entered the tent, and spent our last night enjoying each other's charms. In the morning, we packed, loaded Yofi and Chamor, and walked the short distance to the town.

THE ROYAL CHALLENGE

We entered the square, which was lined with tents and booths, selling food, clothing, some small animals, goats, chickens, and pigeons, along with other items, such as herbs, pretty baubles for women, and of course, money changers, for there were diverse groups of peoples present. We did not know what we were supposed to do, and, so, we stood near the wall, near the outside of the square, and waited, as we held hands. It was not too long before a dark curtain descended, separating us from everyone else. I knew what was to happen, and so I clasped my Nahyim's hand. In a few moments, a cloud appeared in the sky, just above the crowd. Only the two of us were illuminated by a ray of sunlight. Maybe I should have worn my red dress instead of the brown shift.

Expecting some action, I opened my mouth. However, I was surprised to hear a voice from the other side of the square.

"Oh, people of Ashkalon, face the light, I command you."

Frightened, they faced the two of us, and, then, that which I had expected took place. My mouth spoke.

"Your Creator shall speak to you only once. Hearken well, lest you perish. I have seen the manner in which you harass visitors to your city. I have witnessed murder, stabbings, robbery, false measures, and other violations of the Law of Reception of Guests."

Suddenly, there was a stir within the crowd. A group of armed men, surrounding a throne-like chair being carried by four men bearing supporting wooden poles and upon which sat a man dressed in fine robes, were entering the square. Upon reaching the middle of the crowd, this man stepped down, looked around, and spoke in a loud voice.

"Who dares to disturb my authority on a market day? Who are these two, who, I have been told, are stopping commerce. Seize them, and kill them!"

Four of the armed men rushed at us, but, before, they were halfway to our location, a clap of thunder split the air, and they vanished. Then the personage who had given the order was lifted up and up, without any means of support, turned over, and dropped on his crown, with such force that we knew he could not survive. The crowd and the rest of the armed men fell on their faces and wailed.

Once more, I opened my mouth, for I knew there was more to come.

"…as I was saying, when I was so rudely interrupted — because I have seen how guests are rudely treated, rather than being graciously welcomed, I shall give you your law. You shall not covet, nor steal from the stranger within your midst. You shall feed the hungry wanderer, during the stay among you. The stranger shall not be overcharged for lodging and food. The stranger's person shall be free from attack or harm, and anyone who contravenes these laws shall be thrust out of the city. Your law shall be the same for you, and the stranger who lives among you. Should a citizen do intentional harm to anyone, that citizen must pay retribution for the harm done. You shall not allow these laws to be broken, lest I send my fury against you. However, should you obey the laws which I give you, I will ensure rain in its proper season, and you will not see hunger. Learn kindness and justice and mercy for all, and be content. I have given you a curse and a blessing. Choose then, for I do not make decisions for my creations. You have free will. Choose well."

The cloud disappeared, and the sun shone on all. The crowd arose and quietly started upon its business again, not daring to even look in our direction. We went out of the city gates, back to the sands of the sea, put up our tent, and sat. As we sat, I mumbled to myself, although Nahyim could hear.

"Hmm, that is the first time you have acted in such a drastic way, Ayl. It was surely a mighty display of power. Even I was so impressed that I could not utter one word of my own until now. But why so severe a punishment? Surely you could have chastised that person without his having to die. Why death?"

POWER AND RESPONSIBILITY

Nahyim and I sat comfortably, in the shade of our tent, opened up the front and back flaps, and were shaded as the sea breeze cooled us. My question had made Nahyim uneasy, and he chided me.

"Tell me, sweet one, how can you sit there and question the doings of God? How do you dare to challenge what the ruler of the universe does? Are you not afraid of confronting your creator?"

I bestowed an eye flutter upon my husband, took his hand in mine, and explained what I had in my thoughts.

"Dear one, I do not profess to know more than Ayl, nor do I expect my god to obey me. I know how small I am compared to the universe, and that the whole universe is as nothing compared to Ayl Elyon. But you see, I am a human created in Ayl's image — not the body, but my living, my being, and my awareness of creation. Therefore, I must question in order to learn. I must confront in order to understand. I must challenge in order to believe. I do not do this to deny but to affirm and to learn how to be a better image, for that is how I was created."

"Hmm, I understand you, Mimi, but I still would be careful when addressing divinity, don't you think?"

This small side-discussion was broken up by that familiar still, small voice, saying,

"Nahyim, didn't I tell you that your wife had a spark, a fire within her? I have chosen my spokesperson well. As for you, my Mimi, here is what you should know. When a person does evil against another, that person deserves punishment. When a leader does evil and promotes that evil among followers, that person deserves death, because of the harm against humanity, the spreading of iniquity, and the denial of the idea of justice. Where there is no justice, there can be no mercy, no kindness, and that results in evil. When I created all, I saw that it was good; however, with free will came responsibility and desire. My law for leaders is that they should not only do no evil but that they should not even give the appearance of wrongdoing. In the case of Ashdod, there was no hope for the man. He had chosen evil and was leading his people into evil. I have shown the people which road they shall go with their behavior. Let us hope they choose correctly. But that is enough of answering. Look to your Mimi. She is a quick learner. Now, both of you may swim, bathe, and sleep. And when you awaken from your sleep, seventy years will have passed.

"When you have eaten your morning meal, you will pack up and return to Jerusalem, to speak again, in my name. You will mayhap speak to people in high places, but, most certainly, you will speak to one who preaches and teaches, and then you will leave Jerusalem and travel far from home. Again, I assure you that I shall be with you and guard you from harm. For the rest of today, have a good time, rest, relax, and sleep well. I know that you will."

And so, we bathed in the sea and rested, I with my eyes closed. However, I was troubled by what we had heard. What was that about sleeping for a long number of years? I missed my Ima and my brother. What of Chamor and Yofi? There were many questions. I had no answers. Not knowing of how we were to be, we ate well at sundown, entered the tent, and later, much later (happily), as the late-night moon shined down on us, we slept, having faith in the assurance we had received. Our morning was a long way off. When we both woke up, feeling fit and happy, the next morning — or what we thought was the next morning — we did not note any differences with the waves. However, as we walked around the tent and peered back toward Ashdod, everything was changed. It seemed that the town had moved closer to the water and spread out as if it had reached old age. In the tent, there was fresh fruit, pitah, and milk, which we ate, and then decided to go into the town again. Chamor and Yofi looked healthy, and I gave a silent thanks. When we passed through Ashdod, the market square looked larger than before, and there were many more people there. We asked a vendor if he knew any news about the Temple, Jerusalem, or anything else. He told us that Herod had built up the walls, and that the people were unhappy with him and his Roman background. We asked who this Herod was, because neither of us had heard of this person.

"Where have you two been? Have you dwelt by yourselves somewhere in the wilderness? Herod is our King in Judea and was appointed by those pagans in Rome — may the Lord erase their names. Jerusalem is patrolled by Roman troops, and everyone is in a bitter and apprehensive mood. There is dissension among our people. Some wish to appease the Romans and adopt their Roman-Greek customs. Some wish to fight them and rid this land of the pestilence which pollutes the holiness of the Temple Mount, and others sit and wait for a strong leader to help us. There are others who have left the cities and dwell in caves, located in the wilderness. They eat little, do not marry, and pray most of the time — little good it does them. Oh, I must say that, if you do not know all this and are ignorant of what has befallen us, you are fortunate. Look there, beyond the court. Do you see another smaller court, with a building in the middle? That is a Roman worshipping place and contains an idol of one of their goddesses. Oh, it is so disgusting. I must pass it every day, walking to and from my work. It is the same in Jerusalem. Yet, there are some who yet wander around teaching the law and keeping alive our faith in the God of Abraham and Sara, Moses, and the prophets of old. But it is hard, especially for those with young children, who wish to join in games and athletic contests rather than study. Yes, I have a feeling that no good will come of all this. By the way, where did you two say you had come from?"

I thought quickly, for if I told the truth, he would not believe a word. So, I told him that we had come a long way from the South and tried to keep as close to the coast as we could, for we did not want to attempt the southern wilderness without camels. I also told him that we were on a mission to Jerusalem to fulfill a vow.

"A mission to fulfill a vow? What kind of mission? Is it to make a sacrifice so as to atone for a transgression or a thanksgiving for a boon granted by the God of our ancestors? If you wish to make a sacrifice, you must remember to bring shekels only, and, if you wish to make an animal sacrifice, then it must be without blemish, for anything else is supposed to be unacceptable — unless of course, you crease the presiding priest's hand with shekels. If you do, then any beast will do. If you did not know it before, you should know now, that the priesthood has become unclean. Anyone with money can buy the position of High Priest. There are many who are disgusted with the Temple goings on, and there is word that the Romans wish to erect a statue of the Emperor within that holy place. But, enough! I prate too much of things which have little to do with my station in life. But, what of you two? My questions have not been answered, although I have served you with the current happenings. Pray tell, what is your mission — that is, if you may speak of it?"

"We cannot speak of it, unless with permission. Perhaps you may notice some unexpected happenings, and then you shall know of the mission. We however, must be silent on that. I pray you understand." Nahyim replied with a finger pointing at the heavens.

TEMPLE FUGIT

The skies darkened, and — oh, dear — once again, my mouth prepared itself. A loud thundering in the sky drew everyone's attention — and the Lord spoke,

"Hear me, people of the land. Have I not proscribed idol worship? Have I not shown my mercies to all, rather than destroyed? You who have fallen by the wayside and transgressed, behold! Let this be a warning."

A circle of light appeared through a sudden blanket of clouds. There was a perfect circle of light within the midst of these clouds. Then, from this circle of light came a bright bolt of lightning, which struck the Roman temple, throwing its building blocks high into the air, and, when the dirt and dust had settled, the building had vanished in a large puff of smoke. All was still, and then we noticed: The skies were blue — no clouds, no mist — and then came a downpour of rain, on the exact spot where the Temple had stood, but not a drop elsewhere.

The stranger looked at where the roman temple had been, looked at us, and said, "I shall question no more. I have witnessed."

I looked up at the heavens and murmured, "Good job, Ayl. Not only have you destroyed an abomination but have also cleansed it. The more I work with you, the more I admire your style. Excellent job. Well done."

And the answer to my compliment came immediately, in a still, small voice, saying,

"Why, thank you, Mimi, Not since the Great Flood have I done a job as cleanly as this. But, we had to impress the locals concerning certain ritual behaviors, didn't we? I really am not used to this type of appreciative conversation such as I have with you. Formerly, appreciation was in the form of burnt meat, prayer or psalm, sometimes presented with horrible dissonance. However, I have heard you sing as you travel, and must say that you carry a tune very nicely. But we have no more time for chitchat. You and Nahyim have work to do in Jerusalem. There is a young man, Jehoshua ben Yosef, who is going to get into trouble. You must counsel him. He has a very strong ethical strain about him and has quite a following; however, he has not the skill to be a leader. I am afraid that he may not only hurt himself but may make trouble for many more of my people. So, both of you go to the City of David, and I shall then direct you further. Have a good day. I'll arrange that."

And that was that. No more voice. No more orders, except that one. "Go to Jerusalem."

The vendor who had advised us concerning the news was standing and staring at us with a mouth which could have swallowed a whole chicken. He was not privy to the former conversation.

"Never in my life have I witnessed such a wonder. Did you two have something to do with that?"

I looked at him. "Do not worry. That was the work of the Creator. If you noticed, only the pagan shrine was destroyed. It was a warning, and so no one was hurt. But please tell your friends and all whom you value, that Ayl Elyon wishes people to treat each other as family and not to hurt others. The worship of idols does not lead to kindness. But now, we must go. Thank your for your help and information. Peace."

So, we left Ashdod and headed eastward.

WE MEET ROMANS ON PATROL

It takes three days to get to the Holy City, and we would have been there on time, except, after folding our tent on the second day and continuing our journey, we encountered a group of helmeted soldiers, and, when they saw us, they went into the road in front of us and ordered us to stop. We did so, and a tall one with a very fancy shield walked up to us and addressed us.

"Who are you, and where are you going!"

Nahyim told him we were on our way to Jerusalem.

"And what manner of business do you have there?" queried the official.

I then told him that I was on a Vow Mission and must go there. But I was more interested in his mode of dress, so I asked him,

"Excuse me, Roman soldier, but why do you wear such heavy leather clothes and that metal helmet on your head? The sun beats down on you, and I am sure the heat makes you most uncomfortable. Would it not be wiser to wear lighter clothes and just a headband? You would then enjoy the climate much better — don't you think?"

The man stepped forward toward me, bent down to stare in my face, and announced, "Young lady, I have killed men for less impertinence than you have shown me. How dare you question an officer of the Roman Legions! I have a mind to feed you to the dogs. Now, on your knees, and beg forgiveness. Do it NOW!"

"Oh, please sir, do not speak to me in that manner or make me bend the knee to you. I bend the knee only to my Creator, the Lord of Hosts, Ayl Elyon. I must also warn you that if you harm us, you will be punished in such a way that you will never forget it. If you have a family, please, dear sir, for their sake, you must not do anything rash. Just let us go on our way. We have no quarrel with you."

I lifted my eyes to the sky and spoke to the heavens, "Ayl, please do not harm this man. He really does not know the trouble he could make for himself. Treat him gently — please?"

Suddenly, the earth trembled. Where the official stood, a crack opened in the earth, and the crack encircled the officer so that he seemed to be on an island of dirt, and the earth cracked even more, so that he was separated from the rest of the world by a wide chasm.

"Oh dear", I said, "I told you not to menace us, and now see what you have earned. Please, official, just let us go on, and I assure you that you will not be harmed."

The officer's island shook again. Startled and trembling, the officer shouted, "Let them pass! Do not hinder them! Get them away from here!"

And so we went around the chasm, past the group of soldiers standing there with eyes wide as goose eggs, staring at their commander, and continued on our way. As we went further down the road, we once more felt the earth tremble, and, glancing backwards, we saw the officer step over the narrowing chasm to safety.

"Thanks, Ayl," I whispered. "I'm so glad that you didn't hurt any of them. They just did not know with whom they were playing. By the way, you never cease to amaze me with the varied ways you take care of transgressors. It is so much fun to see you at work. I am really glad now to know that you picked me. However, this going back and forth, this constant traveling, is beginning to wear me down. My backside hurts from riding, and my feet hurt from walking. Will a time come when I shall be able to settle in one place and raise a family? Now that I have a husband, I should like to carry out your first commandment to our forebears — you know, the one about 'be fruitful and multiply.' Is that in our future?"

And the still, small voice answered, "After Jerusalem, Mimi, after Jerusalem, you will be sent to a peaceful place where you two may dwell in fullness for the rest of this life. Does that answer your question?"

I smiled and nodded my head, and we traveled eastward toward our destination. We reached the city the next morning and tied Yofi and Chamor to the same place as when I had first been there, and then entered through the huge gate and into the market court. There I followed my nose and found my friend the mocher basar just by following the delicious smell of his kebab on his grill. When we reached the grill stand, I saw that the vendor was not Shlomo but someone who resembled him, and I asked him if he were a relative of Shlomo.

"Oh, I am sorry, but I am Shlomo, and I do not recognize you. I have no other relatives named Shlomo, but my father was Shlomo, and I am named after him. Father died eighteen years ago — may his memory be a blessing. But, I do not know you. Why did you ask me if I was related to him?

Oh, Lord, I thought. *I forgot that the last time I was here was many years ago.* Ayl really meant what He said. How do I give a reply to Shlomo's question? Then an answer flashed through my mind, and I said, "You see, I know someone who knew your father, and she described the location of your stall and what you looked like. When I saw you, I was sure that you were related."

"Aha!" exclaimed Shlomo, "Well, a friend of a friend who knew my father shall be a friend of my whole family. What are your names, and where are you from? Tell me all about it as you taste some of my delectable kebob. Chicken or lamb —which will it be?"

Both Nahyim and I laughed with joy, made our choices of basar, and, as we munched, we told him that we were a married couple with two fine donkeys who had traveled to Jerusalem on a mission.

This interested Shlomo, and he enquired as to the matter of the mission. I hesitated, and as I did so, Nahyim spoke up, saying, "Sweet Mimi, you look tired after our journey. Why don't you go over there and sit awhile as Shlomo and I discuss our vocations with each other. Perhaps, he can point me toward some work, which may be needed." And as I smiled and nodded, he turned to Shlomo and started telling him about being a leather worker, questioning about prospects and engaging in chatter. I took my love's advice and went to a bench and sat and pondered. How should I answer the question?

I AM PROMOTED

As I sat, that reliable still, small voice came and spoke.

"You have experienced much in a short time, Mimi. You have also learned much in the short time you spent with Rav Hillel. Know that you must put your knowledge and experience to work. You will attempt to teach Yoshuah ben Yosef some principles of leadership and give him guidance in public speaking. First shall be the rules concerning how to address a multitude. Make sure that he knows to speak slowly, to enunciate clearly, and not to speak too long. For most speakers, those are enough rules. More important, impress upon him when he speaks of ethics and morality, that he keep it simple. Let him teach with simple stories which will illustrate the point he is trying to make. The tales he tells do not have to be true — just interesting enough so that people will pay attention. Hillel's Rule is of prime importance. Make sure that he understands it. As for my laws, there shall be rules for change. Before any laws are changed, those in charge should look to see if the people will accept the changes and, if so, if the changes will benefit all. Changes should not be made in haste, except in the case of necessity, as when a life is at stake.

"Furthermore, impress upon him that, although nature and all which has been created is very hard to understand, nevertheless, everyone must study as much as they are able, because the more you know of the world, the more you become a great people. Once you are learned in how the universe works, and how humans should act, then the universe will bless you. You should also mention, that birth starts a life, which should be a life of goodness, and that the teaching of the parents must be toward that end. That is the message. You are to teach the young man, so that he can spread this message. You will find him easily. As for Shlomo, you can say to him that your mission is to teach. Shlomo, being a resident, probably knows how your student may be reached. Have a good time, and take your time with your teaching. I shall be present at all times but will not interfere, unless it is necessary to do so. It is that thing about free will. It is your task, and only you can try to accomplish this mission. We shall see what the inclinations of your student will be. Have a good time, and don't get into trouble. But if you do, I'll be there. I'll also see to it that you have restful sleeps. Keep in touch. If you need help, I'll be there."

So I received my teaching assignment.

I went back to where the men were talking about working conditions, taxes, and other matters they could do nothing about, and, when they noticed my return, they turned and welcomed me back. I told Shlomo of my new teaching career, and he looked amused. He then turned to Nahyim and extended the hospitality of his home to us, until we were able to get settled in a place of our own, for property was expensive, he said, and rarely on the market. We gladly accepted the kind invitation and then wandered through the shuk, mind shopping and planning for the future. Everything was expensive. A small rug, fit for seating only two or three people cost the same as two goats or a milk cow. I wondered how we would ever be able to set up a household.

"Oh well," I thought, "Ayl will provide. I've been taken care of in wonderful fashion so far. But I wonder if the task of teaching is going to be easy for me. I've never done it before. Ah, never mind, Ayl seems to have confidence in me. That's all I need. I'm glad to know that the Creator also has faith and believes in me."

We returned to Shlomo's place when we noticed that the vendors were packing up their wares. We helped him clean up, and then he put a top on his grill; placing his carving knife in his belt, he beckoned to us as he started going home. We went for Yofi and Chamor, and all of us arrived at Shlomo's home in good spirits.

WE SETTLE IN

Shlomo's home was not far from the Temple gate and was in a small street off the main road leading up to the gate. It had a cooking-sitting room and two other rooms which served as sleeping quarters. Dvora, Shlomo's wife, looked younger than I and was quite pretty, with long red hair and sparkling eyes. I knew we would be good friends.

Shlomo said, "Hello, honey bee, I'm home. Look, I've brought two honored guests, and what do you know? Nahyim is an artisan, and Mimi is a teacher."

Dvora gave us a long look and, with her hands on her hips, smiled, "Well, don't just stand there, Come in, sit down, and rest. I'll throw some more water in, and we'll have some orange drink and some cake, and we'll talk. So, what brings you to the big city?"

Nahyim spoke. "I am a leather worker and sandal maker. I thought that there might be a temporary living to be made here, while Mimi goes about tutoring her pupil."

"Oh?" and this pupil — he or she must be very important to you. You must be related, or maybe the child is of a wealthy family? What kind of tutoring? Who is this child?"

"Oh, no," I answered, "It is not a child. It is a long story, but to shorten it, I will tell you that, a while ago, I was fortunate to have learned of the law, as explained by Rav Hillel, of blessed memory. Afterwards, I was told that I must contact Yoshua ben Yosef, in order to help him with how to lecture and how to present certain topics. It all has happened so suddenly, in a way, that sometimes I wonder if I am perhaps in a dream. But then, of course, I know that I am not asleep, because here I am, with my Nahyim, and I can remember every moment with him. Oh, I don't know. Sometimes, life gets so confusing."

"Yes, I know exactly what you mean, Mimi. I, too, get that feeling sometimes. After Yaki was born, I forgot the pain and just remember the pleasure of holding him, feeding him, and playing with his fingers and toes. It is also like a dream. Then, when I held him and felt his warm body against mine, I knew I was awake, alive, and happy." But enough talk of dreams and reality and such. Do you know where this Yoshua lives? Did his parents summon you?"

"I do not know his whereabouts at this time. Oh, I forgot to tell you: This is a young man, and, if I do not get to work with him soon, I've been told he will be in much trouble. What can I do?"

Without even a thought, I received my answer from Dvora. "My mother! I am going to see her today and bring her some freshly baked pitah. She hears all the gossip, which travels quickly through this city. Her friends meet daily and discuss the news and what is going on. Upon my return, I will give you all the information you need. Meanwhile, please relax, enjoy your stay, and we'll talk when I get back."

I smiled and thanked her for her willingness to help and for her gracious hospitality. She then left, and I was alone. Nahyim had left with Shlomo, who had promised to show him some likely customers for his leatherwork. I went out into the back courtyard, which was divided into a stable area and garden area. Nahyim had used Shlomo's donkey for carrying tools and leather, so Yofi was left at home. I went to him, scratched him behind the ears, and spoke to him.

"Oh, Yofi, here am I, not even a woman of nineteen years, and I have this large responsibility thrust on my shoulders. Yet, I am orphaned and without family, except for my sweet Nahyim. My vocation has left me without known relatives, yet my husband is still with me, thanks to Adoni, my Lord. And yet, I do not feel too much out of place and as long as I have my Nahyim, Ayl, and you. I suppose I shall be content with whatever befalls me."

Yofi looked at me, gave my hand a lick, and seemed to smile. It was good to have someone I could speak to. In the distance I heard a noise, as of a multitude.

I WITNESS A DISPUTE

I left Yofi, went to the street side of the house, and looked out the door. Nearby, walking in the road, was a group of people, taking a few steps, stopping, arguing with mouths and hands, and then taking a few more steps, stopping to continue the argument, and repeating this strange behavior. There were both men and women there, and I decided to walk behind this group and listen, but I told myself that I must not open my mouth, for I had no permission to speak aloud in situations such as this.

It seemed that they were talking about politics. They appeared to know each other but were split into several camps of thought. One camp wanted to take up arms and throw the Romans out of the Holy City, depose the foreign Herod, cleanse the Temple, and reinstitute proper Temple sacrifice, after ridding the priesthood of those who had bowed to the idolatry of wealth and power. There was another group which cautioned against an uprising and implored all to have faith in the God of our ancestors, who had brought us out of Egypt and given us the Law. There were others who claimed that Yahweh had deserted us and that we were too weak to fight the Romans, so that the best path to follow was that of non-resistance and patience, to wait until Rome got bored with us and left, or until maybe Persia or another empire would destroy both Rome and itself.

I did not know my way around this area, and, when the group turned off into another street, I turned and retraced my steps back home. I had plenty of time to think about what I had heard, but, having knowledge of the nearness of Ayl and the power behind that Name, I had no fear. But I did feel some apprehension when I remembered what I had learned about free will and choices which we alone can make, and I wondered what all of the inhabitants of Yerushalayim would do, if a time came to choose. It was surely a puzzlement. So, I decided to rest. I lay down and slept.

Later, I was awakened by the sounds of movement within the house. I arose and saw Dvora, who had just arrived home. She noticed me and told me to sit down while she told me all the news. Smiling and leaning back to rest, she explained that, after she had arrived at her mother's home, she had enquired about this Yoshua and that "…as soon as I mentioned his name, my mother said that, of course, she had heard of this man, that he had been born in Bayt Lechem. His father was a carpenter from Natzeret, and his mother, Miriam, was a friend of a friend of mother's friend. Yoshua, it seems, had spent some time studying with the people in the caves of Qumran but found that their guiding principles were not to his liking. He had studied the writings of Hillel and seemed to like more the kindliness shown by that sage, and, so, now, he was going around the city, stopping people to tell them about behavior and what Adonai wants us to do. I like what I hear about him, but sometimes what I hear disturbs me."

"Disturbs?" I said, "It must be something very bad, Dvora, because, during the time I have spent with you, nothing has seemed to disturb you. You are the calmest, most gracious person I know. What is it about this man that bothers you?"

"Well, the other day, he ran up to some of the money changers and yelled at them, threatened them, and then chased them away from the Temple area. Now, there is no one around who can change gold, silver, or money from other places, into shekels. Now, every year, when the counting of the people takes place, each must bring a shekel to the Temple. Gold, silver or other moneys cannot be offered. What are the people to do? Also, the rest of the year, if someone wants to buy an animal in order to present a sacrifice, they must purchase it with shekels here. What shall people do if they cannot convert their money? I tell you, this man has created a problem for many of the Children of Abraham."

"He also claims, sometimes, to speak for Adonai, and you know that, to do that is to invite the wrath of God, should that claim be untrue, and, even if the claim be true, some of what he says will make enemies of people in high places and maybe even cause the Romans to meddle in our affairs even more than now. I tell you, something is not right. I fear the future. But enough of my fears and talking. I must prepare for the evening meal."

She got up and started working. I excused myself. told her I needed to get some air, and went out. The animals in the back of the house welcomed me, and I greeted each one with a pat or smile and sat down on a stone bench, which rested under the lone tree in the yard. Sitting there, I thought about what I had just heard and then remembered the dispute of this morning. It seemed that maybe the two were related somehow or that there was a kind of questioning by many of the people about what the current state of affairs was. Could it be that the children of Israel were no longer a family? Were they splintering into different groups? I had to find out more about what was going on. Oh, dear. My head was so full of thinking that I could no longer reason.

MY ADVISOR AND COUNSELOR RESCUES ME

Then, sitting there, a thought came into my head. What if I went to see this Yoshua tomorrow? What if I spoke to him and tried to find out what he was saying, what he thought? In order to teach, I would have to find out where his mind was and what he knew or believed. As I was mulling this over, the still, small voice returned, much to my relief.

"I see you are trying to plan your venture, Mimi. Glad to see you working, even before you meet your student. That's the sign of the good teacher — preparation. But, I must tell you that there may be obstacles to overcome. You see, he has a following of quite a few people. He also has some men who accompany him wherever he goes. Seldom is he alone. You will have to be careful, because, among those mentioned, there are those jealous of his time and attention and, frankly, do not admire interlopers. Some of them have had some experience with those Essenes, who live in caves, where the men shun the women, and the women shun the men. This might be troublesome for you. But, do not worry about them. When the time is right, I will arrange for Yoshua and you to be able to converse. After you introduce yourself to him and tell him of your history, he will then make time to see you on a regular basis, and then you will be able to talk. Be careful. I do not trust his band of sycophants. Some of them are there only because of his public repute, and, so, they see themselves as part of his reflection. Many of them misunderstand what he says, and I fear for him. Oh, well. They will do what they will do, and you will do that which I tell you. We will see. I have faith in you and your mind. Not only do you have a quick way of reaching a right conclusion, but you also have a sense of rightness in behavior. I watch as you talk to Yofi and how you care for him. Anyone who has room in their heart not only loving her own kind but to love the world is my kind of person. Truly, I made you well in my image. Now, tomorrow, go you out there, find your student, and begin your task. I shall not desert you, and neither shall I fail you. Got that?"

"Oh, Lord! I hear you, yet I'm slightly shaky. You know how it is — the first time you try to do something? You don't know how it's going to turn out, and you wonder what if...?"

"Ha! Tell me about it. When I first pondered humanity, did I not wonder how it would turn out? I'm still wondering. You know, this free will thing is extremely dangerous to the whole world. It can be used for good or bad. People can choose to build or destroy to be kind or to be cruel. It is a two-edged sword, which can enrich people's lives or destroy them. In granting this, I reserved the right to interfere only with messengers, like you. In cases such as these, I interfere only when my emissaries are threatened. I shall not allow you to be hurt. So, Mimi, knowing all of that, are you ready? Go out there, and fight for what is right. Let nothing stand in your way. Are you with me?"

"YES!" I shouted, and, jumping up, I ran to Yofi, untethered him, took him out to the street, and we slowly charged onward.

I LISTEN

Oh, dear. I was so excited by the conversation that I had forgotten I did not yet know where I was to go, and then it came to me. Ya had said that I would be guided. I looked up, smiled, and whispered,

"All right Ya. I know. You're on the job." I loosened my grip on Yofi's reins and relaxed, and, looking all about me and taking in the sights, while Yofi decided where to go, we forged on. He walked from the upper city, took a few turns, and ended up in a courtyard outside the Temple Wall. As usual, there was a crowd selling food and animals, and, in one corner, just as there was in the courtyard below as one entered the city, a raised stone platform. There was a man standing and speaking, but I could not hear what he was saying, so I paid a vendor of fruits to watch Yofi. Nearing the speaker, I could just make out what he was saying. There seemed to be a question about the penalty for certain transgressions of the law. He looked at the person who, I assumed, had brought up the matter of a son cursing his parents. The speaker was denying that the words really meant what they said — that the child should be taken outside of the city or town and that all the inhabitants should throw rocks until the child died. In a clear voice and speaking quickly, the speaker said,

"…Yes, I agree that the cursing of one's parents is a major error, a Chait, a missing of the mark in that it shows not only disrespect for the parents but also disrespect for the whole community and its laws, thereby showing disrespect for our Creator, who rescued us from Egypt and gave us that law. But tell me, for the past one thousand years, since we left Egypt, have you ever heard of this penalty being carried out? Have you, yourself, witnessed such a deed? Of course not, since it has never been recorded in any of our annals. This law was put in the Tora as a warning that the fifth of the Ten Commandments was to be upheld and to put the fear of the Lord into children. No one expected that it would ever happen that parents would cause their child to be killed."

"I tell you here and now, that, when you read the law, our Torah, you must look for that which you can do to make this a better world, a place where everyone may live together respecting each other and ensuring that the City takes care of all — not just the wealthy — for it is not the wealthy, who love their gold, who are held in esteem and love, but those among us who love all humanity as they do themselves and thus do nothing to hurt anyone. I tell you that the commandments, even the negative ones — those which say 'Thou shalt not....' — even those should be studied in a positive way to look for the end result of the meaning. We should teach the children not only that they must not covet, nor steal, nor murder but give them reason not to transgress the law. But, my brothers and sisters, we are here for only a short time, and we may say to ourselves, 'But what can I do, being only one person, without power? What can I do to help make this world a Gan Eden?'

"I answer you thusly. You will do what you must; otherwise, your life is without meaning. You live and you die, just as any animal, and then who will remember you? Who will mourn your death? For your own sake, you must keep the law in your heart. Before I leave, I shall tell you that if you cannot remember the whole of the laws, then remember this: A good person is that person who will do nothing to harm another, just as that person would not wish to be harmed. To harm another, to hurt another, to speak evil of another is to kill something inside the other. That is the prime law. It stands atop the pyramid of all the statutes, ordinances, and commandments, which have been recorded. I leave now and bid you all a peaceful and fulfilled life."

And he started to walk away, followed by a small group of mostly men. I hurried back to get Yofi, and then we both went to follow the speaker and his group.

CALL ME YOSHI

As Yofi trotted down the street, following the group, I wondered that we might get lost but decided that, since Yofi knew that he was to follow the group, he would remember how to get back. Finally, the group stopped at a small clearing, which had flowers and shade trees. I noticed that the women, who I thought were with the group, were no longer present. The men sat down to rest, and, as they sat, I tied Yofi to a nearby tree, which had grass growing near the trunk and, leaving him, approached the group. As I got nearer, one of them noticed me.

"Look!, a woman approaches. Shall I chase her off? Why does she wish to bother us? I am sick of these mooning cows following us. We have better things to do than to dally with them. Go away, woman! We have no need or your presence, your talk, or any services you might wish to offer. Begone!"

I was shocked. Never before, had I been addressed thusly by a descendant of Jacob. Was he not one of us? Was he Roman, a pagan?

"How dare you address me in such an unmannerly and crass tone! Have you no manners? Who are you to tell me what I must do? Did your mother not teach you how to greet strangers? Have you forgotten that you, yourself, were a stranger in Egypt? What have I done to you that you treat me thusly? If you cannot endure my presence, then I suggest that you leave this place, thus easing your pain, for I intend to stay and then leave at my pleasure, not yours!"

As I finished, the rest of the group set up a howl of laughter and ridicule which caused his face to turn a fashionable red. When I saw his embarrassment, I quickly added, "Adon, I apologize for my sharp retort; however you must realize that you, yourself, were rather sharp with your tongue, and it, indeed, hurt my feelings. I trust that we will not, should we meet again, have to address each other unkindly but rather as fellow humans who would not wish to hurt one another."

He took a step back, as if he could not believe my words. But what could he say? It appeared that I had disarmed him. Then, the man who had lectured spoke up saying,

"Well said, stranger. Soft words can avert strife. You have done well. Come and join us. Have a seat. We are about to dine on bread and cheese. If you wish, you may partake. Come. Join us. We shall introduce ourselves."

As I sat, he continued, "My name is Yoshua ben Yosef. I was born in Bayt Lehem, not far from here, and I visit different places in order to learn, to study, and to tell others of what I think. These men, here, are also doing the same, and we search for answers to some of the most difficult questions which can be posited. And now, who are you? And why are you here? Oh, by the way, I did notice you back there in the square, although you did hang back in the crowd. You seemed to be paying very close attention. Were you that interested in our discussion, or was it just curiosity? Pray tell."

"Well," I said, "my name, at one time, was Batya; however it was changed to Mimi a while back. I am a teacher and was drawn to your talk because it echoed some of the same ideas that were taught to me by my teacher. I found it refreshing that someone else had either studied his works or had come upon these matters independently."

"Oh?" said he, "and this teacher of yours — would his name be known to me? Where would there be an academy in which girls and women learned how to explain the law? Who was this learned sage?"

I was suddenly caught up in confusion. If I told them I had studied with Hillel, they would laugh, for I looked no more than a woman of twenty years, yet Hillel had already been dead for a while. They would take me for a spinner of stories, and, being a woman, it would even make it worse. They would never take me seriously. And then it happened — Ya came through again. There was a clap of thunder and out of a blue sky, came heavy rain. We all arose, fled the open space, and looked for shelter. I ran to Yofi, untied him and led him quickly away. The group ran in all directions. As I was running off, I heard footsteps behind me but did not bother to look, since I was looking for some sort of overhang for shelter. I finally found an archway and stood there, only to be joined by the owner of the footsteps — Adon Yoshua ben Yosef himself. We both shook ourselves off, and, as we stood still, Yofi walked around me, went up to Yoshua, and, looking him in the eye, just nodded up and down and then went back to me.

"What was this all about, Mimi? What does this mean — first the rain and then the donkey inspection? What does the donkey mean by the stare and the nods? Perhaps you can tell me?"

"Well, first of all, since we have met, you may call me a friend, and I hope that we can be study friends. As for Yofi here, he just likes to inspect people I meet for the first time, in order to give me an indication of whether he approves of them or not. He is a very good judge of character, and I trust his judgment. You saw how he nodded. He approves."

Yoshua laughed, walked to Yofi, patted him, and scratched him behind both ears. "Thank you, Yofi. I really appreciate your approval. You are wise beyond your ears." Yofi looked up and brayed loudly as if to laugh at Yoshua's joke. "Yes, Mimi, I do believe we can study together, the three of us, and maybe we can make some sense out of the chaos of life. By the way, my close friends call me Yoshi. Please do so yourself."

The rain stopped. I looked up and whispered, "Thanks, Ya."

Yoshua heard me whisper and asked, "What was that? You thanked Adonai — for what? What is this? Who are you? This is very strange."

I looked around. There was no one within hearing, so I explained. I told him that I had been sent to tutor him in the craft of speaking in public and that this was my mission in life thus far. I added that, for the moment, I could not tell him any further details but that they would eventually follow and that he must trust me. He heard and looked a bit doubtful. I did not know how much I could tell him about myself at this time. Then I had a plan. I said, "Yoshua, my new friend, hear me out. I shall leave you here for a few moments. When I return, you will know that I speak the truth."

I left and walked not too far away; once more, I called on my Rock and my Guide. "Oh, Ya, how can I ensure that he believes me and trusts me. What can I do?"

As soon as my questioning was finished, the answer came.

"Thus far, Mimi, you have done well. I liked the way you handled the rudeness which welcomed you. Good job, girl. Now for the signs and wonders. When you return to the arch where Yoshua awaits you, you will invite him to step out into the square. Then you will ask him to slowly turn around and tell what he sees in the sky. He will see nothing. Then tell him to do it once more. That is all. I shall be seeing you. You can be sure of that."

And, just like that, the conversation ended.

Signs and Wonders — in Color Yet!

I walked back to where Yoshua was standing and beckoned to him to come with me. We stood in the middle of the square, and I told him to turn around and look at the sky. He did so and said "I see a cloudless, beautiful sky with sunshine warming the back of my neck now."

"That's right, Yoshua. I see it, also. Now, close your eyes for just a second, and then open them and turn around. "

Yoshua smiled. I knew that he was thinking that I was just joking with him, for what did a twenty-year-old girl know? However, he smiled and indulged graciously in my request. When he opened his eyes and turned around, both he and I could see a glorious complete circle of a rainbow over the entire Holy City. It was magnificent, and yet there was no cloud and no sign of rain anywhere.

"What kind of witchery is this, Mimi? Are you one of the forbidden? Please tell me that it is not so. I know that rainbows are usually seen before or after rain. This is the dry season, and, although there was a cloudless rain a moment ago, there is no sign or hint of rain now. What have you done?"

"Oh, Yoshua, don't be afraid, and don't think ill of me. All you see before you is the work of Ayl Elyon, our Creator. That which you see in the sky is a sign from Adonai that he is pleased with us and wishes us to continue our conversations. I told you that I had been sent to help you. Now, settle down, and I shall tell you what has been told to me. Do you wish to listen now, or do you wish to do it tomorrow? It is your choice, since you are the student, and my only work is to teach you. Then I shall leave; so choose, because the sun will set soon, and I have to go down to the upper city, where I lodge with my dear husband, Nahyim."

"Your husband!" Why did you not say so, before? You know that it is not wise for a man to meet a married woman without witnesses. Your reputation is in danger, Mimi. We have to stop meeting like this."

I bridled at what he said. How dare he impugn my reputation — and aside from that —

"You listen to me, my fine friend, and you had better listen with both ears, because this is the first lesson. Now! Do not ever, again, insult me in such a way. After what you have seen, do you doubt that we have a very reliable witness? Is not your God witness enough? So, I tell you now, that whatever I teach comes not from my head, nor is of my creation or thought but that which has been either taught to me or commanded of me. I do that which I am told by Ya. Do you not think that I fear for myself should I ever disobey? I have seen the wrath of God and the suddenness of the punishment, and, so, I am quite happy to humbly obey that which is commanded. Do you understand? Have you taken in my meaning? Have I made myself clear?"

Poor Yoshua hung his head, saying nothing for some moments, and then spoke in a very, very quiet voice,

"My sincere apologies, Mimi. You must understand that I have never experienced that which happened just now. My first thoughts were that this was unbelievable and that, therefore, you must have bewitched me. I feel now that I was mistaken and that you are truly an emissary of the God of Jacob. I pray that you forgive me and that we may continue our discussions. I am truly sorry. I shall not doubt again — and please call me Yoshi. But since the afternoon grows late, would you like that I accompany you and see you safely home? "

"Dear, dear. Still doubting. But, first things first. To clear up any misunderstanding about our relationship, let me be clear. I may learn something from you; however, that which I teach you, you must take to heart, so that you may "prophet" from it. (Of course, we were not speaking English, so he did not catch the pun that I threw him. It is lost in translation.)

"Secondly, no, you may not see me home, for that would be a denial of my protector's promise and power. I am safe no matter where I go or where I am, for the Creator is with me. Thirdly, I think that you must absent yourself from your friends for a while until we are finished with our lessons. We must learn six days a week, and I do not wish to teach on the Sabbath and keep you from studying the law at public services. I also wish to spend some leisure time with my patient, loving husband. I shall meet you tomorrow at the Temple gate to the upper city, and, then, I shall bring you to Shlomo's home, where we can study together. That will be the schedule. Meet me just after the sunrise prayers. Is that convenient for you?"

"If that is the way it is to be, I shall do what you suggest. Tomorrow after morning services, at the gate to the upper city. I shall be there. But, what of now? I think we should be on our way, because it will be dark soon. I am not a native here, so I must see in order to wend my way to my lodgings. So I shall bid you Shalom, and L'hitraot — to our next sighting."

"Lyla Tov, Yoshi. See you tomorrow, bright and early." And I got on my Yofi, and we started back to Shlomo's house.

As we started off, I heard Yoshi's voice once more, "Shalom Mimi — it has been a wonderment to meet you."

And that was that — so far, so good. Everything was arranged. I looked up and whispered, "Thanks, Ya. You made that quite easy for me. I just love the way you decorated the heavens. It is really a shame you did not just leave your art in the sky. It looked like a crown for the Temple. It was extremely imaginative, yet simple in array so as not to be vulgar. Impeccable taste. I'm glad I was there to see it." I really didn't expect an answer, but, lo and behold, it came.

"Ah, the teacher is now an art critic and commentator on decorative design. I am most delighted and pleased that you approve of my signs and wonders, Morah Mimi. I am also pleased that you say what you think and feel, for, usually, when people talk to me, I know that there is always a part of them that they wish to hide. This repression of guilt prevents truth in conversation. But again, it is a human's choice. I do, however, wish they would get over it. Many problems would not arise if people followed the laws of decency. Well, teaching that will be your job and, later, Yoshi's labor. I certainly hope he can carry his work out. But, let me not slow you on your way. Drive safely, and I shall see to it that you have a good night. Lyla Tov."

And that was that. I arrived home just as the last of the daylight was fading. When I walked in, the three of them jumped out of their seats with such a commotion, I could not hear the words. Finally, Shlomo raised his hand and shouted "Sheket!" — which made me laugh, because he had shouted the word for "silence," and his voice had been the loudest.

They settled down and were quiet for a moment, and then Nahyim spoke, "Oh, Mimi. We were so worried. We did not know where you were and did not know where to look. You just disappeared. Where were you most of the afternoon? We saw that Yofi was gone, and, so, we felt that you had gone to the market, but when you did not return, we were so worried that some mishap had befallen you. You must never do that again, only because of the anxiety I feel when I do not know where my love is. But never mind. You are here, now, safe and sound. So, please, if you can, tell us about your day. It must have been some important business you were on, to disappear like that. Please tell us."

And so, I related some of my day's doings, leaving parts for later, when Nahyim and I were alone, for I did not have permission to disclose everything to my new friends. At the end of the telling, I asked permission of my hosts to use their back lot as a tutorial studio. They laughed and said that they would have no objections. They added that I could use the kitchen table whenever the rest of the folks were away from the house. I was delighted and thanked them.

After the evening meal, we went to our bedroom, and, then, I remembered that I had not seen to Yofi. I jumped up, ran outside, and saw him standing there, waiting patiently and pawing the ground with a front foot. I quickly dumped some hay in front of him, placed his bowl of water nearby, and scratched him behind his left ear. He turned his head, gave me a quick, light love bite on my arm, and I bade him Layla Tov and went back to Nahyim, who was sitting up, waiting for me. After lying down, he put his arm around me and said, "Well, what is the rest of this adventure? I know that there is more to your telling."

So, I told him about all the rest and asked him if, at any time in the afternoon, he had noticed anything strange in the sky. He said that he had not, so I told him about Ya painting the sky. Nahyim sighed and told me that he wished he had been there, for it must have been something wondrous to behold. I answered that he was right on the mark, that it had really been wondrous. I then said that the next time I spoke to Ya, I would ask him that, at a propitious moment, Nahyim might also be allowed to see another of the Lord's beautiful artistic creations.

Then I said, "Nahyim, this is something new. I didn't know you were interested in art. How does a leatherworker become a devotee of the artist's work?

"Ah, my love, I have traveled all over this land of ours and seen many beautiful sights, from the water springs at Banyas to floating in the Salt Sea without sinking. But, as for works of humans, do you not think that, as a leatherworker, I am interested in design and pattern? It takes craftsmanship bordering on artistry to design a bag or belt, or even a sandal. I have been to a Beit Teffilah where the mosaics on the floor were beautiful works of art. Flowers and animals and designs flooded my eyes. Oh my adored one, you are not the only one who is stunned by beauty. In here, right now, that is my condition as I feel your nearness. Oh, how I love you, and am grateful to Adonai for the accident of our meeting."

"Accident? Accident? You call that an accident? Hmphhh! That was no accident. Although Ya doesn't interfere in our choices, nevertheless, we are assisted or aided in mysterious ways. Our chance meeting was, to my way of thinking, arranged. Ya had told me that he would take good care of me, and, when we met, I had a feeling that you were the one I was destined to love. I did not know how you felt until later, my love, but all's well that ends well." (He could not catch the reference because he had no knowledge of the Bard. But I thought that this bit of plagiarism was apropos — do you not think so?)

But Nahyim seemed troubled. "Oh, yes! It has gone very well thus far, but what of the future? Will this love-filled life of ours continue thusly? I always hope for the best but expect the worst. Look at the conditions in our land. We are ruled and controlled by pagans. Our people are in disarray, and our political and economic situations are no better. I fear the future, my love, not for myself, but for you. If anything bad were to befall you, my life would be over."

"Oh my sweet Nahyim, look at me. I have no fear. We have the best protection in the world. No one can do mischief to us, for both of us are on a mission for the Ruler of the Universe. How much better assurance of safety do we need? Whatever happens, you and I are going to be together for a long, long, time — longer than you can imagine. Now stop thinking dark thoughts, give me a kiss, and let's get some sleep. I've had a tough day at work." and so we slept.

THE BEGINNING OF SCHOOL

My eyes popped open before sunrise. This greatly surprised me, because I seldom awoke during the dark time. I was also immediately aware that I did not have the drowsy after-waking-up feeling. I felt rested and ready for the new day. I quietly arose, not wishing to wake my husband, washed and dressed, and went to eat in the dim glow of a lamp, which I carried with me. I suppose that every house had one little oil lamp in every bedroom, as a nightlight. Anyway, after eating, just as the sun was rising, I went out to Yofi, who brayed for me to feed him. I gave him a hug and brought him some hay. I had brought just a little bit of honey from a little clay pot I had purchased in the market and poured some drops of it on the hay, as a special treat, because today was to be my first day of formal teaching. I was so excited that I could not be still. The anticipation of what was to come made my insides announce that they were still there. My heart beat a little faster. So, I decided to do something that I had omitted for a while. I went over to Yofi and started to sing to him. Again, King David's songs were pleasing to the animals, and, when I came to the last "Let the whole heart praise Ya," Yofi joined in, the hens cackled, the rooster crowed, and the nanny goat added her alto along with the lamb's bleat. The chorus resounded, and, when it ended, and a bit of quiet returned, I heard a voice.

"Well done, Mimi. I have not heard such a splendid morning service for a long time. You are a splendid leader. My trust in you grows as well as my admiration for your talent. I am ready to hear what you have to tell me. Where shall we learn?"

I felt my face turn a bit red and felt slightly abashed at being found singing with animals; then I thought to myself: "Why should I be ashamed? I did nothing wrong. In fact, I was doing the right thing in choosing the songs and singing them. If my friends, the animals, chose to sing along, why, that was their business and no one else's!"

I turned and said aloud, "Good morning, Yoshi. I am glad that you are here in time for us to have a full day of talk. I am also happy that you appreciate the music my friends and I produce. I am sure it makes them happy, too. But, enough of exchanging pleasantries. Let us go to that bench under the tree and start."

We sat, and I started with, "First of all, my mission is not to tell you how to think, but rather to tell you how to invite others into your way of thinking and to speak to them so that, rather than just hearing noise in a crowd, they hear and listen to you alone. Are you in accordance with what I have just said?"

"Why, Mimi, I tell you that I shall hang on every utterance of yours and take it to heart. You shall find me a willing student. Please."

And so we started. It went something like this: I told him to stand at a distance from me and speak for a few moments. When he had finished, I told him that he must not let his words tumble forth from his mouth too rapidly, because, when speaking to a large crowd, it is imperative that one speak slowly and clearly, enunciating every part of every word. One must speak loudly enough so that the people farthest from him would be able to hear every word clearly. Again and again, he spoke, and, before the noon meal, he had developed a rhythm and speech pattern which showed great improvement. I then told him that he must personalize whatever he says and must not seem to be staring into space. He should focus on a person in the middle of the crowd and imagine that this was the person he was addressing.

After the midday meal, when we continued, I told him that he should speak to the motley crew which had surrounded him when we met. There were one or two of them who had eyed me in a very distressing way. They looked me over from head to toe and had a look on their faces which was, to say the least, unpleasant for me. Yoshi was to warn them that dire consequences would ensue were they to follow their desires, instead of minding their own business. I was in no mood to banter in the way of giggling young girls. We had some serious business to attend to.

Yoshi looked at me as if I were some type of creature he had never met before. In a quiet voice, he said, "I shall so inform them, Mimi. Whatever you say. Only please, have patience. They sometimes forget their manners. They are young, and I gathered them out of the gutter and rescued them from homes which were not typical of Judah. They have much to learn before they are fully grown. But I shall keep them in check. I'm going, later in the afternoon, to the square and try out my new public-speaking technique. This has been a good beginning, and I am grateful to Adonai for sending you. I am also beholden to you for all you have taught me today. If there is anything which I may do for you, please tell me, and I shall see to it. But tell me, Mimi, you do not look as if you are old enough to have had all the experience and learning which your teaching exhibits. Why is this? What kind of person are you that you possess all this wisdom? You know, of course, that you are a most puzzling and mysterious person. What is this power which you emit?"

I smiled at him and thought to myself that I would have to discuss these questions with Ayl. I did not know if I should burden him with my responsibility for my silence.

"Yoshi, Yoshi," I sighed, "You ask too much at once, and I do not know how to answer. One thing I can tell you is that I am a simple countrywoman who has a mission, and, if Ayl grants it, you may someday share that which has befallen me. For the time being, be content to know that not only has our God favored me but also that I have the impression that you are also favored. Keep the faith, Yoshi. Keep the faith. That's enough for today. Go and mull that which you now know, and plan what you have to say, remembering technique and enunciation at all times. Have a good time, and don't forget to advise your colts not to kick their heels too high."

Yoshi looked at me as if he had another mouthful of questions but succeeded in swallowing them. As he bade me Shalom and thanked me again, he left.

I took a deep breath, leaned back against the tree, and whispered, "Dear Ayl. I am completely exhausted, yet I have hardly moved since awakening. This teaching is much more strenuous and tiring than laundry, or cooking, or anything else I experienced before now. Is this how I shall feel every day from now on? And what about Yoshi's questions? Shall I tell him all, some, or nothing? He surely is a curious type yet seems to be quite quick when it comes to learning. What shall I do? Please advise as soon as possible."

No sooner had I finished my bakasha (in English, 'my request') than I received my answer.

"My, my, Mimi. You are in more of a hurry than your ancestors were when they left Egypt. Please be seated, and bring Yofi to sit next to you so you may stroke him; this will release the anxiety and tension which besets you currently. I shall counsel you in due time, so that you will know how to proceed."

I went to Yofi and, untethering him, led him under the tree, motioned for him to lie down next to my bench, and seated myself. He looked at me with a questioning look, and, then, as I started stroking his neck, he lowered his head and fell asleep. Within moments, I began to feel my neck muscles loosen, and I felt much more comfortable.

GOOD NEWS, BAD NEWS

After relaxing with Yofi, I went indoors, and Dvora came in from visiting her mother and shopping. She told me that, in the square where she bought her vegetables, she had seen a personable young man standing and talking aloud to a huge crowd, who were listening intently. I interrupted her with a cry of delight, feeling that Yoshi was the speaker and was using what he had just learned. But, then Dvora continued and told me that next to her had been some men, richly clad, who were grumbling and complaining that he was a public nuisance and that something should be done about him. Wondering what these men could be talking about, I decided to take Yofi and ride to the square to listen in. We arrived to hear a tumult, and, in the middle of this was my student, Yoshi, who appeared to be having some difficulty in being heard. It also seemed to me that some unfriendly people were shaking their fists at him. I asked a woman standing nearby what was happening.

"Oh, it is just one of those young rabble rousers who's attacking the priesthood, and the rich and famous. He says that it is a transgression to ignore the poor and pay homage to the wealthy. Well, what can you expect from this generation, all wild-eyed and idealistic? No sense of reality. Oh, well, he'll grow up, and, if he doesn't, the world will teach him a lesson."

Immediately, I excused myself, went to a corner of the wall, and whispered, "Dear Ya. It looks like trouble for Yoshi. I cannot handle a crowd like this. Without intervention, he may be hurt. What shall we do? I do not like the sound of this crowd."

There was not a word of answer. Suddenly, out of a blue sky, there was a clap of thunder, and rain poured down upon the crowd, wetting everyone as if they had jumped into a pool of water. Then came lightning and more thunder and more rain. Within one minute, the square had only two persons standing there, both dry. Yoshi and I were the only ones left. He looked about him, dazed, and then he saw me. The rain and noise had stopped, and, as he neared, he recognized me and said, "Mimi! What are you doing here? I thought I had left you back in the yard. What is going on?"

I laughed, but not too loud. "I heard that there was a commotion here, so I came to see for myself. I assume that, after the sudden rain, you raised your eyes to the heavens and thanked Ayl Elyon for his refreshing shower. After all, very few people can claim to be cleansed by the Almighty when surrounded by unsavory conditions."

"Ayl Elyon? What do you mean, Mimi? Are you telling me that you know something of the Lord's doings? Who and what are you? I have seen and heard some very strange goings on when you are in the vicinity. Please. I am more and more puzzled and confused. Explain why and how, precisely, you have come into my life."

Once again, I had to go through the whole routine. I told him to go sit somewhere, to leave me alone, and that I would join him shortly. He complied.

After he left my side, I turned around, so that he could not see my face, and whispered, "Well, what's the next step?

What do I tell him, if anything at all? The poor boy is bewildered and seems to be losing it. Advise, please."

"'Advise please'? 'Advise please'? Anyone besides Mimi would have said, 'Please help me, I pray you,' or something to that effect, but my Mimi asks for advice, as if I were her minister of state or religion. Ah, Mimi, I chose rightly. You are spunky and perky. Now, as to what to tell Yoshi. Tell him all, and if you wish to leave out anything, that is your choice. Of course, he must, under no condition, tell anyone of what you disclose. Tell him that I would consider it a serious breach of confidence, and I don't hold with that kind of behavior. Now go ahead. Tell him your story."

"Now Ayl, are you sure you wish someone besides Nahyim to know this story? You know that a secret is not really a secret if more than one person knows it. The more people who know about this — well, I don't know if that is a good thing."

"Well, I am Ayl, and I do know a good thing. Now go and do as I said, unless, of course, you wish to be rained on, in order to clean your thinking out. Oh, Mimi, sometimes I forget, when you try my patience, that you are only human. Go now. We're still friends."

So I went and rejoined Yoshi, who was sitting on a bench, looking glum. I started my narrative with my childhood and brought him to the present. I included Nahyim, Yofi, and my long sleep, and the interventions of Ya along the way. I pointed out that it had been only Ya who could produce the downpour out of a cloudless sky. As I finished, Yoshi looked at me with big eyes and said, "I have been in the presence of the God of Abraham, Isaac, and Jacob and did not know it. I have been truly blessed. Baruch Hashem (Praised be the Name)." Then he grew silent.

"True," said I. "You have been not only in the presence of but also have been saved from a nasty business by your Creator. Now, tell me: What was all that commotion about? What did you say to stir up the people?"

"It was the same thing I always say. Things like 'Rich people should see to the poor and the widow and the orphan. That the Priests should not accept payment for accepting rotten animals and grains for sacrifice' — things like that. What was different this time was that I used that which you taught me. I spoke clearly, slowly, and loud enough so that people farthest from me could hear. I do not know what turned many of them against me."

"I know," said I. "It was probably the first time that the people really heard what you had to say. Some of them might not have liked it. We will have to work on how you present your material. Remind me tomorrow morning, and we'll see what we can do about that. Well, the afternoon is waning. Go home. I'll return to Nahyim and meet you tomorrow, same place. When do you think you'll arrive?"

"Probably mid-morning, Mimi. Is that convenient for you?"

"That's fine, Yoshi. Oh, one more thing which needs no further comment. No one else is to hear my story which you have just heard — not a parent, not your closest friends. If you have a lover, speak not a word. What you have heard is for your ears only and for no other. I warn you that any deviation from this directive will be most unpleasant in the consequences which follow, and this message is not from me, but I think that you may infer the source. I do not demand a vow from you because, vow or no vow, your lips must be sealed on this for your own well-being. See you tomorrow. L'hitra-ot."

I turned, went to Yofi, and we trotted home to await the next day. Arriving at home, I discovered that the others had preceded me and that, once again, Nahyim had been worried about my going to where trouble was brewing, for Dvora had told him. I pulled him into the back yard, where we could be alone, gave him a big hug and kiss, and reassured him that I was never in danger. He still did not understand what a protective shield had been constructed for me. It is not that I was fearless but rather that, after all that had befallen me, I knew I would never be deserted in a moment of need. I tried to convey this to Nahyim, and he said that he understood. Yet, in his eyes, I could see that he was still in a troubled and anxious state. I then decided that, as soon as my mission and work were finished, I would no longer be anything but a loving wife and mother, and would grow old gracefully together with him. Then the question arose — When would this time come when I would no longer be a working wife? Then another question arose — When that time did come, would I be content to just stay at home and not experience the excitement of the outside world? And then I said to myself that I should not bother with these questions since they had no answer. I would deal with them as they arose.

I took my husband's hand and led him on a quiet walk, just to enjoy each other's company. We hardly spoke, but there was a string, a rope, a something which could be felt but not seen, and seemed to be connecting us — something that went beyond words. We were feeling each other's companionship and love, and that was all we needed. I thought myself so lucky and silently sent an inward psalm of praise and thanks for the gift of Love which had been bestowed upon us.

GETTING THINGS STRAIGHT

The next day, both Nahyim and I awoke at the same time. We greeted each other, as usual, and afterwards, still had time for small talk.

"Well, how did it go yesterday? Did your student learn anything of value? Tell me what is new in our lives."

"Oh, Chabibi, it's funny you should ask. I watched him as he talked to a crowd in the square. Total disaster. He spoke slowly and distinctly, and the people were able to hear his every word quite well. That was the problem. They understood what he was saying. However, his topic grated on the ears of many. That's when some of them grew quite unruly and threatening, and so there had to be an intervention. You should have been there. Out of the clear, blue sky, there came such a drenching downpour that the square emptied before you could say Todah L'Ayl (Thank God). I do believe that, without that assistance, there might have been violence done to poor Yoshi. I think that today we will discontinue our lessons in 'slow and distinct and concentrate on how to say what is to be said. He sounded like a judge who was sentencing all of them. I do not think that people like the idea of someone pointing out their faults directly, especially in public. We'll concentrate on how to reason with people so that they understand the point of discourse, without being insulted or angered. I'm so glad that Rav Hillel was able to take time to sit with me and learn how to present a problem so that it may be understood by even a child — but more important, how to deal with that problem in such a way that no one feels pain. Oh, how I miss that man."

"Excuse me?" interrupted Nahyim, "Exactly what do you mean by 'how you miss that man'? Exactly in what way do you miss him? I am not jealous, of course, but I must know what you mean."

"Oh, Mohtik (Sweetie), the man was ancient when I met him. He had a beard long enough to have served as his clothing. No, it was his mind which I miss. He had a way of talking about the law which made one admire the law for itself, because you could understand how it fit into our relationship with others and with the world. He had a way of taking the most intricate statute and pulling out the simple truth and meaning behind the wording. His knowledge of the history of the traditions behind the law and behind the customs, was very great, and he used this knowledge to explain how each commandment fit into the growth of human relationships. Oh, how I miss him. "

"Ah, dear Mimi, I see now the reason for your sighs. I have really never met a woman who longed for a person because of the mind. But then, I am only twenty-four, and my association with women, before our first meeting, was usually limited to leather goods and sales. Yes, I see now that you were fortunate to have had a wise and wonderful teacher."

"Just a moment, young man! What is this with this 'usually limited to leather goods and sales'? I distinctly heard that word 'usually,' and it disturbs me. Could you please explain those instances in which the association with women was unusual? What kind of unusual relationships have you had in the past?"

"Well, my dear, if you must know and are really interested, I'll clear this matter up right now. When I was five, my first playmate was a neighbor daughter. We grew up together and were very good friends until she turned twelve or thirteen and lost interest in me. A few years later, she married a miller and moved away. Later, during my travels, I met a woman, a widow, not much older than I, who had come to order a pair of sandals. She seemed to be very interested in me and came to my stall every day, although I had told her that the footwear would not be ready for two weeks. She was not from Judea but was the widow of a Roman merchant who had died here. When she made an offer to me, I could not bear to hurt her feelings, so I lied, saying that I was already betrothed, and could not break my troth. She understood and left me alone until she picked up her goods. That was the last time I saw her. Then, up to the time of our meeting, I was too busy traveling, looking for markets, and making a living, and that is the extent of my association with women, other than my family and business dealings."

"Oh dear, Nahyim. I hope I haven't hurt you with my questioning. I confess I felt a little jealous when you spoke of other women, but now I know there was nothing to worry about and no need to bother you with that sort of thing. Thank you for your honesty, and, now, give me a kiss, and let us be about our day. We have to eat the morning meal, and I have to get ready for my pupil, while you have to go to work. Up and greet the morning light."

I jumped out of bed and danced my way into my clothes humming and singing. Nahyim arose and also dressed, as he smiled and watched. At that moment, I knew that I was the happiest, luckiest woman in all of Judah — and maybe even farther. Afterwards, I went out and saw to Yofi and the rest of my friends, fed them, provided them with water, and we sang a chorus of Praise. Then, inside, our host and hostess joined us, and we ate.

EVOLUTIONARY ELOCUTION

That night, as we lay in bed, I had tried to sleep, yet couldn't help wondering how best to help Yoshi grasp the skill of teaching with simple words, simple ideas, without angering those who were there, yet winning them over to his side. Then I remembered something which Hillel had told me about a Greek slave who had taught many children and adults some very important life lessons. This man, Aesop, had made up stories which illustrated situations in real life and then showed the consequences of choices made by the characters. Most of the time, the characters were animals, which was sure not to disturb people. Yes! I would show Yoshi how to create situations which were a source of learning yet would not cause anger among the listeners. Smiling, I cuddled up to my Nahyim and slept.

The next day, when Yoshi and I were once more on our bench, I started to explain to Yoshi that there are many ways to communicate with people.

"You see, Yoshi, a mother may say to you, as a child, something like "Get away from the fire NOW!" knowing that you could hurt yourself. However, a stranger, seeing you play with fire, might not be so bold but use other words to achieve the same result. Can you think of a way to say that to a child?"

Yoshi thought for a few moments and answered, "Well, I could say, 'A fire can burn and hurt you very badly. It is not a toy. Does your mother know what you are doing?' That would stop the child for a moment, I think. Or, I could say something like, 'Fire is not for playing!' That, I think, is slightly stronger, but I really do not know whether that would stop a child who is fascinated by flames."

I then turned to him. "Both examples were very good and, with an understanding, older child, might very well prevent pain. Suppose you told the child a story about another child, an imaginary one, who was playing with fire because the flames were pretty and wanted to see how close his hand could come to the pretty colors, when suddenly a tongue of flame touched his clothes, and thus caused him such great pain that he could not sleep or eat or drink for many days and suffered much pain for months. Maybe that might work better. The more interesting and dramatic the story, the closer will the listener pay heed. The first thing to remember is that you must initially get the listener's attention. Next, you have to set the scene in which the problem is presented. Finally, you must make the listener wonder how the story will end, and that is where you make your point or your moral, the end result of your lesson. The listener, hearing your tale, can then relate the events to real life and learn how to make ethical or wise choices which do no harm. That should be the core of your teaching. Before good may be done, one must be assured that no harm results from any actions. By the way, did you know that this was the central point of all of Hillel's teachings? "

Yoshi said no words for a while. He just sat there with his chin in his hand, leaning over his lap, deep in thought. Finally, he looked up. "I think I have it. Make it a story which mimics real life. Inject a moral problem, and then resolve it by teaching an ethical precept. Ah, so simple. When I think of how the prophets of old spoke to the people — mostly with harsh indictments and scorn — I wonder how many of the people were so insulted and downcast that the main message went unheeded. Fiction painting life. What a marvelous concept. I shall try it out today. But what shall I use as an example? How about opposites? You know, slow-fast, up-down, love-hate, war-peace, greed-munificence; those kinds of things are all timely subjects."

"Yes, they are, Yoshi, but don't forget to personalize your stories, whatever the subject. The people listening must be able to relate their own lives to that of which you speak. For instance, 'slow-fast' could be a good background for loss of temper, or deciding how to deal with foes, or even how to answer a loved one in a conversation. Slower, in those cases, might be better than fast. But, look at the case of someone who is drowning. That is not the time to introduce yourself to that person, and ask from whence he or she comes, is it?"

"Oh, Mimi, you make my mind bright with light. I have today's topic. There were some people grumbling about some Samaritans who were in the market today. They were saying how the Samaritans should stay on Mount Gezirim and stay away from Jerusalem, because of what happened four hundred years ago. They reported to Nebuchadnezzer that we were rebuilding the walls of Jerusalem and that we were plotting a rebellion again against Bavel (Babylonia). This was untrue; we finally prevailed, and there has been enmity between us ever since. There is nothing more sneaky and treacherous than those Samaritans. I have an idea for a tale which will instill in some of my listeners the idea that hatred may not be good nor that the "other" should always be an outcast. Yes. I shall tell the tale of a good person who happens to be an outcast. Let us eat some lunch now. I have brought some food for us to share before I leave for the square. May I pour?"

I agreed. We ate. He left. I sat quietly for a while and wondered how he would fare in his lecturing this day. Then, my curiosity caused me to rise, and, taking Yofi, we went to see my student perform.

Even before I entered he square, I heard his voice clearly, engaging, and, as I walked into the square, I saw the crowd, quietly listening. He was talking about ideals of pity, feelings for the other, including everyone as a child of the Lord, and the act of kindness as a commandment, and not simply a good voluntary deed.

"You have been told by the sages that, if you save the life of one person, it is as if you have saved all of humanity. Is there no greater good than the saving of life? Yet, why then do we differentiate one life from the other? I shall tell you a story, and you shall be the judge of actions. On the road to Jerusalem for a pilgrimage festival, one of the travelers became ill and fell by the wayside. Everyone on the road was in a hurry to get to the Holy City, and so they paid the fallen person no heed. He just lay there. A passing person who was not on pilgrimage, a Samaritan, noticing the stricken pilgrim and rushing to see what was wrong, immediately gave the sufferer water to drink and supported the pilgrim until both were standing. Then the Samaritan helped the pilgrim until they had reached the city gates many hours later. By that time the pilgrim was rested and could go on alone, and the Samaritan, refusing any reward, bade goodbye, turned around and went back from whence he had come. Where in this tale lies righteousness? Does the rush to offer sacrifice overshadow the need to come to the aid of the ill and suffering? There are some who would say that the Law demands a clear barrier between right and wrong, but, when confronted with real life, they cannot see because they are blinded by belief. Were we made for the Law, or was the Law made for us? When we stood at the Mount and shouted, 'We shall obey, and we shall listen,' were we intended to read the law blindly, without understanding why it existed? I tell you that the law has, as its foundation, the relationship of one human to every other human and that perfecting that relationship connects us to our relationship with our Creator. It is only what we do to make a better world that will justify our existence. That is our prime task in our few years here. Can the rich man take his flocks and property and wealth with him when he dies? I say that, truly, the Lust for Gold is the root of all that is bad, and that the love of all creation is the root of all that is good. Therein, my friends, lie our choices. Choose Life and Good. Praised be the Name of the Lord."

Not a word was uttered, and you could hear people breathing. Then Yoshi, having seen me, descended from the speaking rock and came toward me. The crowd parted as he moved. I walked out of the square to where Yofi was waiting, and Yoshi joined me.

"I am utterly exhausted with my speaking. Never have I experienced such a fatigue. Yet, I note that no one seemed to be angry at my words and that there had been no interruptions. I hope that they understood my message. I hope that I got through the tough skin of my brethren."

"Don't worry, Yoshi. You did fine. I saw that you had all of their attention and that they were listening for your next word, your next sentence. It appears that you have learned all that I can teach you. I am so glad that I was the one who could help in this matter. But now, let us change places. I shall walk the rest of the way, and Yofi will be glad to assist you. He also is a good donkey, probably from Shomron (Samaria)."

Yoshi roared with laughter and doubled up so that he almost fell over. He finally caught his breath and told me that he would be honored to have the assistance of Yofi. He mounted Yofi, and we continued toward Shlomo's home. I knew very little about my student, so I asked him, "Why is it that you know more about me than I know about you? Before we get to Shlomo's home, I want you to tell me about your life, your family, your travels, and your wishes for the future. Just talk. I shall listen."

And, so, he started talking. He told of his father, a carpenter who hardly made a living, what with all the taxes, tithes, and expenses. His mother Miriam was a very kind and gentle lady who worked hard to make a happy home back in Natseret, where they lived. He had been born when the family was on its way to the Temple for the Passover offering. He felt that this trip had affected his mother in a bad way, and he worried about her health. He also told me that he had been searching for meaning in his life — that he felt that there was more to life than just being born, existing for a while, and then dying. There had to be a reason. He said he had been searching for answers. He had spent some time with the Essenes in Qumran but had left, because they rejected the world and divorced themselves from the rest of humanity, waiting for the world to end. They said that they wished to purify themselves and that this could not be done mingling with the ritually impure. He could not accept their lack of love for all of Creation, and he opined that they had missed the point of their own lives' existence. Yet he still had no answers to his basic questions. As he put it, "Why was I born? What gives meaning to my existence? Why am I here?"

So young, so deep. For a moment, a shudder of fear went through me. I felt that these questions were not to be answered in this world, for people's worth can be measured only by their life's deeds. Should he continue this quest, he might be led into dangerous paths. But, as we neared home, I turned these thoughts aside, and, knowing that the poor boy was tired — and certainly hungry, I ran ahead and asked Dvora if she would mind having a guest to the evening meal.

"Did you ever hear of Abraham or Sarai saying 'No' to a guest? Did any of our ancestors ever turn a weary or hungry traveler from a meal or a bed? I do what I must, because it is in my blood, Mimi. Show your guest in. He is surely welcome."

As Yofi came to a standstill and Yoshi dismounted, I asked him to join us for a meal and immediately told him to hush and be still when he demurred out of courtesy. I grabbed his arm and pulled him through the door. After he was seated, I ran to Nahyim, gave him a squeeze, kissed him on the nose, and introduced him to Yoshi. Then I bade him meet his hosts, and we all sat and supped. After cleaning up, we went out to enjoy the cool evening breeze in the back. Sitting there, Yoshi once more related what had, of late, befallen him, and my hosts, as he spoke more, looked inquisitively at me but said nothing. When it darkened, Shlomo insisted that Yoshi stay over so that he could return when daylight appeared. He pulled out a straw-filled mattress from somewhere and set it up in the kitchen as a bed for Yoshi, and we went to our rooms. In bed, Nahyim whispered,

"Seems like a nice person. A little idealistic and impatient with the world, but I guess he may learn that a person cannot change the world overnight, or in a lifetime, or in many lifetimes — that is, Mimi, except for you. Isn't that right my love?" and he nipped my ear.

"Oh, Shecket, you tease! I don't know what you mean — and keep me out of this. No more teasing. You have to take me as seriously as I take you, and, when I take you, it is very seriously." And I lightly bit the back of his neck. After a while, we slept.

RAMPANT PHILOSOPHY

The next morning, we all arose and ate the morning meal, and then Yoshi thanked Shlomo and Dvora for their gracious hospitality and told us that he was going to meet with his "study" group because he had missed several sessions with them while he was studying with me. He asked me if I would accompany him and teach something of my choosing to his fellow seekers.

I cast my eyes at Nahyim, and he said, "Go on, Mimi. I guess that's part of the job. You can't wear a sandal until all its parts are joined. They probably need you." I sighed, because I really wanted to stay with Nahyim but decided, against my better judgment, to do as Yoshi had asked. Once more, I kissed Nahyim and left, to accompany Yoshi to his session.

Unlike the eve before, this time I rode on Yofi, and Yoshi walked. We discussed several topics which might interest the group, and Yoshi decided that we would raise the subject of stone throwing, because the group was composed of young bachelors, and, when they spoke of others, it was sometimes in disdain and disparagement.

"I have to get them to the point where they see that they do not have all the answers and that other people may know things which might be useful in terms of understanding others and the earth itself. Yes, today, we'll play with rocks."

"Sounds like a good place to start, Yoshi. Erect your verbal temple, and see who enters willingly. However, I think that I should tell you how I feel about the group. While you are with them, see how they relate to one another. You know that within each family or group, there are always people vying for leadership. Also, there are people who act as Shadchanim (mediators or facilitators) and try to bring people together in agreement. There are also the naysayers, who will have nothing constructive for the group but will always disagree without resolving anything. There are all kinds and types within a group. Learn to recognize each type, so that you can learn how to deal with all situations and people. Hillel taught that a kind word would almost always turn away wrath and that anger begets anger. I have a feeling that your stature as a speaker in the community will grow as you gain experience, but you must always look behind you to see who your followers are. People have a habit of taking the spoken word and bending it for their own purposes. In this way, as they continue to twist words, they can change a Yes to a No, or Love to Hate. Speak carefully and admonish your group that if they accept your lessons, they should not deviate from your words. That is most important. How does that resound with you? Does it make sense? Can you understand how it may have an impact on your future?"

"Ha!" laughed Yoshi, "What future? Here I am, with the whole world seeming to tumble about me — Romans defiling the Temple, Priests buying their office; all around us impurity, lack of trust. What future do any of us have? I see no future in this life. Like Jacob, I wrestle with my Creator. Where is the promise of the Promised Land? Where is our Gan Eden reborn? Where is our milk and honey? Why do we suffer? Are we all like Job — leaves of a tree, destined to be blown away and eventually turn to dust? Did Hillel tell you the answers to these quandaries, these quick sands of thought?"

"Before I attempt to answer you, I heard you mention this man Job. Tell me what you know of him. Where does he stay? What has he done?"

"Oh Mimi, it appears to be Greek or Persian, I am not sure — a sad tale of a righteous man who had everything one could wish for: family, property, flocks, herds, everything, and he walked humbly with his God, was charitable and kind, and yet, he was completely and suddenly made bereft of everything, family and all. His friends came to comfort him, yet he would not be comforted. When they accused him of pride, he denied pride with good cause. When they said he was being punished for transgressing the law, he denied the indictment. It seems there was no reason for his misfortune. All of this comes from a tale which has circulated and has been written down. It sounds to me as if it is of recent origin. Now that I have told you about Job, can you answer my questions? If so, I'm listening."

My head was reeling with the impact of his speaking and questions he raised. But I thought of Hillel and what he had taught me about Aesop and some of the other Greeks who were thought of as great teachers — Aristotle, Socrates, The "Cave Man" Plato, Archimedes — the Man who wished to have a long stick in order to move the Moon. All of these, along with our sages, had provided me with a treasure chest of knowing. So, I started slowly.

"Yoshi, think back to beginnings. Did not the Creator say to us, among other things, '…have dominion over the beasts of the field….', signifying that we were the rulers of our world? Then later, in the holy Torah, did not the Lord give us a choice? If we obeyed The Law, we would be rewarded and would be satisfied, but if we did not, we would be punished. You, yourself, have said that people today do not obey the law — neither rulers nor priests nor the people of the land. When this kind of social order of greed and disobedience of the ethical and moral code which the Law implies is the ordinary course of social and business dealings, then, what would you expect — milk and honey? Of course not!

"So then, your question of our purpose here on earth becomes a problem for society. It becomes questions of, 'Why are WE here? What is OUR purpose?' If you wish to search our Torah, you will find that our purpose is to re-create the conditions of Gan Eden. It is an ethical directive to help Ayl, who has given us this world as our realm, to help finish his job of Creation. Remember that God did not work on the seventh day. It is a day of rest. It is a day for all those who are free to contemplate our condition. We must allow all humans to become more human and less animal. More in Adonai's image, in that our imagination, our creativity, and all our purpose is to ensure that the whole family of humans may live together in peace, in cooperation, considering no one to be outside our tent of hospitality. When all humans can gather under that tent of goodness, then and only then, shall we know why we were born and be happy, because of that. Until that time, it is up to us and the children to come, to learn about the world and its people, to learn how to work within the world without hurt to either world or people and to ensure that the word 'hurt' may, sometime in the future, disappear for lack of necessity to use it.

"As for Job, the tale you tell me of the discussions of Job and his friends puts me in mind of the books of the Greeks, who have discussed these topics. Some of them conclude that there is no God, and so the best that one can do is have a good time with the time we have. There are some who say that there are gods who play favorites among people so that they prosper, while others do not. The Greek philosophers could play with these theories because their gods were created in the image of humans, with all the strengths and weaknesses which we ourselves have. So, as they observed all the people around them, they imbued their gods with cunning, sloth, cruelty, jealousy, and all the other attributes which humanity possesses. That is why these great thinkers could develop theories for our being here as well as for what befalls us.

We, on the other hand, believing that there is only one God, one Creator, and one Law, can, with the help of our own sages and thinkers, create a philosophy which makes sense of Creation, Life, Death, Sickness, and all that our existence entails. This Creator which we have is the only God of all who is an ethical deity. Therefore, if this story of Job had been written by one of our sages, the ending would have been that all that Job had had before his misfortunes, he got back at the end of the story; yet being human, he still did not understand the meaning of his life, because he could not picture the whole of the universe from beginning to end. If we accept that Law, then we have a clearer picture of, what the world and we are all about. It is not that we should live as if we have finished our work but to live to work for that day when all people reside in a just and kind world. When Hillel stood on one foot and told the pagan that the Law was 'That which is hateful to you, do not do unto another. That is the Law. All else is commentary' he took the whole Torah and all the commentaries and reduced it to those three short sentences. Yes, indeed, all of your discussions, all of your debates with your fellows will gain you nothing if you forget Hillel. As you asked, I shall go along with you today, but only to see if you are ready to stand on your own two feet alone and deal with questions and attitudes."

"Sounds reasonable, Mimi. Thanks for that answer; never has the light shone for me as quickly as it did today. You lifted the mist from my thinking and showed me a path which I can willingly walk.

"There, just outside the city — you see that grove of trees with benches? That's where we are meeting. They are waiting."

We approached the group, which numbered less than a dozen, and, as we neared, I heard, "Oh, here comes trouble, again."

PHYSICAL PHILOSOPHY

We reached the shade of the trees. There were ten of them grouped in a circle. Yoshi greeted them and re-introduced me. "You remember Mimi, from last time, don't you?"

There was a mixed murmur.

"Why does she have to be here? It's impossible to have discussions with women around. They have no mind for deep subjects. They are all involved with feelings, emotions, and such. They belong in the kitchen!"

One of the men arose and answered him. "Yehuda, you speak shtuyot! (nonsense). There are women who study. There are women who are learned. Had it not been for your mother, would you be here, or would you be out on some field, naked and throwing an iron ball or spear in the air? Be calm, listen, and then judge another person's worth by what they say, by what they do, rather than what you think they are. Now, I beg you, sit down, and relax. Open your ears, and let your mind be a sponge to soak up the waters of knowledge!"

"Well said, Matti (short for Mattathius), said Yoshi. But, enough of this squabbling. Today we shall talk about rocks. I would like Mimi to introduce the subject."

"Rocks!! You mean large stones?" shouted Yehuda. "I thought we were discussing the law, not agriculture or carving. What has law got to do with rocks. Is this a joke? Is this Mimi here to entertain us? If so, I should prefer her belly dancing to rocks."

"Now, just one moment, Yehuda," shouted Mika-el. "Let someone else get a word in. Maybe you can learn something from another speaker. Stop interrupting, lest we become angered. We're here to learn."

"So what if someone does get angered? What has that to do with me?" retorted Yehuda, "I frankly don't care what someone else thinks, especially you, Mika-el. I'm tired of you always telling me to be quiet and to listen and to learn. I know what is good for me, and, as for you, see to yourself and take care of you, for no one else will do it. No one cares for your soothing of souls, of your quiet approach to problems. I for one, feel that when you are faced with a problem, you solve it and then discuss it afterward. Now stop bothering me, for you are a problem, and if you don't cease, then I shall stop you. Do you understand?"

There was an uproar. Yehuda and Mikia-el rushed at each other and started wrestling and punching each other. Yoshi tried to intervene, and a stray fist brought bleeding to his nose. It was as if a war had broken out.

I looked up and whispered, "Ayl! Should I do something? What can I do? I know that you probably don't wish to intervene, since this is not a world-shaking event, but I do feel that what is happening is not a good thing. Answer, Please?"

Back came the reply. "Walk over to them, tap them both on a shoulder, and step back. The fighting will end. Go now."

I did as I was told, and the second I touched and stepped back, the two mighty warriors fell backwards and sat heavily on the grass. It was as if they had pushed each other unexpectedly and bounced off each other. It was rather comical to watch, and the onlookers pointed and laughed at the two champions seated in opposition.

Yoshi again stepped between them and said, "See! The result of this behavior is that my nose is bloodied and hurts. Both of you should know that before you act, you must think of the consequences of your actions. Rushing to do battle usually results in injury to innocent people. Do you believe that this is what a good life demands? What is it with you two? Have you lost your way in life? Stay where you are. We will start our discussion for today, and the rest of us will sit in a circle around you. It is hard to talk with all this blood in my throat and mouth, but, should I falter, I am sure that Mimi, my good friend and tutor, will continue. Is that understood?"

Except for one or two under-the-breath mutterings, there were nods of agreement. So, Yoshi started his story.

"There was once a woman who had three children. Her husband had gone off on a long journey for trading purposes. He had left her a little money, but, as time went by and he did not return, she was left without the means to feed her children. A neighboring man who saw her plight made her an offer. If she would play the wife with him, he would see to her and to the children's well-being. After a long struggle with her beliefs and conscience and seeing her children starving, she agreed to his terms. Many months went by before the husband returned, and, finding out that his wife had been unfaithful, unheeding of her explanation, he went to the town officials and accused her of infidelity. A trial was held and the verdict was.... And that is the problem, gentlemen. What is the verdict and what shall be done?"

From the center of the circle came the voice of Yehuda. "The law is very clear. Any woman who is guilty of adultery, and there is the evidence of several reliable witnesses, why, she shall be taken out of the city gates, and the citizens will stone her to death! Where can there be any discussion? Where is the problem?"

Yoshi looked around and asked, "Does anyone see a problem here? Is there something out of place? Is this the proper application of the law?"

The circled group looked at one another without answering, as though waiting for someone to challenge the law. Then someone stood up and said, "I should like to speak and ask some questions. May I?"

"Of course, Shmu-el," replied Yoshi.

"Well, we might wish to ask, first, if the husband was innocent in this whole business. He was, according to the story, a merchant, and he must have known that he would be away for a while, yet left his wife and children without sufficient means to continue living. Is it any wonder the woman did whatever she had to for the sake of the children? Does he not also bear part of the burden of guilt? Also, the neighbor had the opportunity to lend the woman money for necessities with the expectation that he would be repaid in full when the husband returned. Did he not even think on this? He took advantage of her. She saved the lives of her husband's children, and would you have her put to death on that account? These are only some of the questions I have. I also have a question about the law itself. It is true that she committed adultery if we look at that law, but there are other laws which claim that almost any law may be broken to save a human life. Why, you may even force a dying man to eat pork to save his life. The fasting on the Day of Atonement may be broken to save a life. Is there a way to look at both of these laws as equally just and make adjustments to our thinking? I would suggest that maybe those who would throw the stones might not do so, were they to think of those times in their lives when they deserved equal punishment. Of course, Yehuda, you sound as if you would be glad to cast the first stone at the woman. Yet, think: She saved three lives by doing something which she must have detested. Would you be so innocent that you would cast that stone? Answer me if you can."

I could no longer hold myself in. I looked at Yoshi and saw that his eyes were on me, as if he were expecting me to continue, so I did.

"Shmu-el, you couldn't have said it better. Aside from the neighbor, did not others not know of the wife's plight? Did no one in the village notice that her children were hungry? Did they not notice the absence of the merchant? If justice and its carrying out is the responsibility of all the citizens, isn't it also the responsibility of all to see that no one goes hungry? Was it not the looking away of her neighbors which added to the woman's misery and which forced her to do something which was wrong but which was the only road she could walk? If we take Hillel as a guide — and for those of you who have studied the ancient Greeks, I shall include the great thinker Hippocrates — society and all its citizens must first of all obey Hippocrates when he gave the first rule of medicine to the Medical Profession, which is 'Do no Harm.' Hillel, after studying Torah for many years gave us a similar law: 'That which is hateful to you, do not do unto your neighbor.' He also added to this: 'That is the law. All else is commentary.' If you remember nothing else from today and retain only Hippocrates and Hillel, your life will be richer. You will not be the first to throw the stone. You will be engaging in your true work — that of making this a better world. Please remember that, for, after today, I shall not meet with you again. I have other work to do. Yoshi, go get some water, and wash the blood off your face. Mika-el, I suggest that the next time someone picks a fight with you, utter soft words. It is better to speak softly and make a friend than to speak harshly and make an enemy. That is only an extension of Hillel's rule. It may be applied in almost every instance when people are together. It is also the way you magnify the name of Ayl Elyon, in whose image you are created. I bid you a peaceful and fulsome life. Shalom."

I walked away toward the courtyard and neared the fountain where Yoshi was almost finished tending to his insulted nose. Aside from some bluishness in his skin and redness around the eyes, he seemed to be progressing toward good health.

"Yoshi," I said, "It is time for us to part. I think you are ready to become the leader of your pack. Remember to treat them gently, but beware of what might go on behind your back. There are, maybe, one or two of them who seem to be ladder climbers. They do not see where they are going, but they do not wish to be at the bottom but rather at the top, looking down on the rest. Beware of those who profess to love you and lavish you with praise. They are up to no good. Look for the humble, the seekers, and those who search for truth in the law and who do not study it for personal gain or for study only. This study must lead to a better person — otherwise, it is vanity. May God, the merciful and all-powerful, be your shield, and may you not be victimized by those you love. Shalom."

I walked to where Yofi was standing and left for home and Nahyim.

THERE'S NO PLACE LIKE HOME

I arrived at Shlomo and Dvora's home in time to join Nahyim in the backyard, where he was sitting with his tools, stretching a leather hide over a wooden frame. I asked him what he was making, and he told me that he was making a tabletop for our hosts, as a gift for their hospitality. "What a wonderful idea, Mohtik (sweetie)," I said, "and it will be so handy. I see that you've used olive wood for the frame and legs. That table will last for generations. What a wonderful present. I grabbed him and kissed him, murmuring in his ear "Oh, how I love you, you marvelous human, a gift from above, for me."

He dropped his awl and stretching tool, gave me a hug, and laughed. "Oh, Mimi, I was not sent by heaven. I was on a trip, going south, just happening to pass by. Maybe Ayl had something to do with it, but don't forget that this kind of fortune happens to others, also."

I dissented. "Oh, no! We were meant for each other, and our footsteps were guided from birth, my innocent puppy. I have a feeling that this marriage was made in heaven and that we have been blessed like no other humans, except maybe, Adam and Eve, or, or — I can think of no others. Yes, you and I are unique, and don't you ever say that other people are as fortunate as we. They may have love, but not our love. Don't you ever forget that." And I wagged my finger in his face. How dare he question the heavenliness of our marriage? Others, indeed!

"I was not questioning anything, dear Mimi. I was just singing your praises and praising Ayl, in a sort of roundabout way. Please don't misunderstand, for I am not blessed with the gift of language that you have been granted. I am but a poor leather man, unworthy of this royal marriage. Look! I bow and beg your smile. Make your servant happy, and bestow an upward curvature to your lips. Let sunshine radiate from your visage, and let poor Nahyim bask in its glow."

"Oh, well said, faithful servant, and, so, I shall grant your request; however what shall I take in return, for the effort of moving my facial muscles? Yes, I shall demand a physical encirclement of my torso by your arms as soon as you have finished your basking in my glory."

And so we bantered with each other, as he worked, and I watched him. He asked me how the morning session had gone, and I told him everything that had happened. When I had finished my telling, he stopped working and turned to me, saying, "You know, Mimi, from all that you have told me and from what I have seen of Yoshi, I am fearful for him. He is a good soul, completely innocent of the outside world and its dangers. I have a feeling that the future holds not much in the way of good for him. From what you tell me, I think that some of his friends do not have the stuff of which good people are made and are not true friends. Yet, who are we to interfere in others' lives? You have done that which you were told to do. You warned him to be careful. Whether or not he chooses to obey your words is up to him. May Ayl guard him. But, now that your job is finished, why don't we go back to Kinneret and settle down there close to where you lived before? Perhaps you still have family there. What do you think about that.?"

"Oh, yes! I had always dreamt of that, as a youngster — to live in a home close to the water, with the one I loved, surrounded by twenty children. Oh, yes. Let's leave today."

Nahyim laughed. "Slow down, slow down. It is a trip of three days, and twenty children is not a family. It is a herd. Think small when you think children. Now we have to pack. I have to finish this table, and we have to say our farewells to our friends. I think we can be ready in two days, if you can do some of the packing and gather provisions for the trip. How does that sound?"

I settled down to married reality, thought about it, and told him that two more days would not be a tragedy. I would get started immediately. That evening, after all of us had supped and cleaned up, we were sitting around as Nahyim and I told them of our plans and told them that, if they ever traveled north, they should enquire after us, and we would be able to show them around, while they stayed with us. Dvora agreed to go shopping with me the next day, in preparation for our leaving, and Shlomo said that we were the nicest visitors they had ever had, including even his in-laws. At that, Dvora glanced at him and said,

"Hmpphhh. That younger brother of yours and his wife are no bargains, either. Always complaining about lack of enough spices in the food, the size of our hen's eggs, the street noises — and you complain about YOUR in-laws."

They looked at each other and then at us, and the four of us burst out laughing and started a whole new conversation about married love and in-laws, and spats about the little things which go on in married life. It was an interesting conversation, which ended when we talked about how nice it was to make up after a quarrel. My only afterthought was that I regretted not having any in-laws or extended family. I guess I shouldn't have done so, but I could not help but quote from the morning lesson, as I told them "As Hippocrates said, 'Do no harm,' and, as Hillel said, 'That which is hateful…'". At that point I was interrupted by three voices, which finished the Rule and provoked more laughter.

The sound of our glee was such that an onlooker would have thought that we all had overindulged in a firing up of the Hookah and strange smoke. As the hour was growing late, we said our good nights and retired. It had been an eventful day, and I was exhausted but happy.

The next day, Dvora and I went to the market, where I purchased some staples for the trip, matzah instead of bread, because pitah would quickly go stale, figs, dates, eggs packed in straw, some olive oil, and anything else I could get in the way of provender. It should have occurred to me that there would be opportunities to purchase food along the way, but I wanted to be sure that Nahyim did not go hungry. Dvora stopped off at another stall and purchased a beautiful lace tablecloth, which must have cost one-half of a sheep, at least. When we got home, she turned to me, gave me the purchase, and said, "Dear Mimi, Shlomo and I want you two to have this table cover to use for your Shabbat meals. Every wife needs to beautify the table on which the wine and Challah are placed. Use it in good health."

I started to cry. I couldn't help it. The joy I felt just swamped my feelings and expressed itself as tears. Dvora enwrapped me with her loving arms and told me that she understood. She had felt the same way when her mother had presented her with the same kind of present. It was a very special moment, which I shall never forget. It also reminded me that I had never had a chance to see my own Ima, once I had left, and that she was no longer alive. I then knew that, just as Ayl had somehow arranged my meeting with Nahyim, so had my meeting with Dvora been no accident. The meeting had been set up, but the friendship was because Dvora was a very special person, a kind of big sister, sent to be a sort of mother, to fill in for the one I had had to leave. It is hard to be contracted for the work of the Lord. Oh, well, nothing can come of brooding about the past. We have only the present and the future, and the present goes quickly. So I went to join Nahyim, told him of our gorgeous present, and, after pillow talk and such, we kissed once more, and we slept.

We spent the next day in preparation for the trip. This time, unlike when I had originally left home, the packing was leisurely, with time taken to have a picnic lunch in the back. We finally had Yofi loaded and our bundles on our backs, and off we went, after getting assurances from Dvora that she would somehow get all the gossip and news to us, whenever she heard of someone traveling north. That eased my apprehension a little bit, for I really feared for Yoshi — he was so innocent and unprepared, yet I knew that I had done whatever had been told me. He knew as much as I about public speaking. Then, we left, and my mind turned to our trip and return to Kinneret. Oh, how I longed to bathe in those waters again. How I wished I could feel the cool evening breeze and lie there waiting for the moon — this time with my Nahyim. These thoughts made me feel good, and, with each step, I knew we were closer to our special place.

We stopped off once more, at Bayt Shahn and, within two and one-half days, had arrived at the southern shore of Kinneret. Never had water looked so beautiful to me. Never had the flowers along the shore been prettier. We stayed there for the noon meal and ate some fresh fish that Nahyim caught. The fish were sweet, and we could see them swimming, just offshore. The next morning, we arose early and arrived at Tiberias, a small town, south of where I had lived as a girl. We stopped to do some shopping and eating, and got to where my home had been, a long time ago. The little house was still there, and, when we enquired, of the owners, they told us enough so that I could identify them as cousins. It appears that they were the grandchildren of my brother. I, of course did not tell them that. Who would believe my story? I still looked young. I told them that their mother and my mother had been related and that we must be distant cousins. When they heard this, they welcomed us, and we entered my old home. It seemed strange to see all the walls I had once known. Some of the decorating was different, and I could see that, even though I recognized my walls, they no longer recognized me.

"Oh, well," I thought to myself, "I have lost a home but gained a wonderful husband. I have been extremely fortunate." Looking at my Nahyim sitting there, smiling at me, I felt so loved, so warm and comfortable with my being, that I had to hold my arms down on my lap, lest they start flapping and I would fly around the room. Was any woman so lucky as I?

At that point, Nahyim spoke, addressing our cousins, "We appreciate your kind welcome, cousins, but Mimi and I must find ourselves a bit of land and think about settling down. If you do not mind, we shall take a temporary leave of your company, and we hope that, as soon as we know where we are and what we are about, you will favor us with a visit. I would also ask that you please send word to your friends and neighbors that there is now a leatherworker in the community and who is a highly skilled artisan who can shape a tabletop, a saddle, a set of reins, sandals or leather adornments engraved with fine art. We both thank your for your kindness and your friendship." He gave them both a hug, as if they had been his cousins all our lives. I followed his example, and, when the affectionate farewells had been accomplished, we left and trekked northward.

After a day and a half, I turned to Nahyim and said, "Where are we going, my love? I no longer know where we are, except that the Kinneret, over which I could see the other side, is now much narrower. I have never been this far north. Where are you taking us?"

"Oh comely, vivacious, lovely woman, I had the good fortune to have been this far north once before, and I know of a place which shall be our home. It is a place of rare beauty, perfectly fitting for my Malka Mimi (Queen Mimi)." And his eyes twinkled.

We reached a place where I could hear a gurgling noise, and, a few steps farther, my ears recognized the sound of water. We rounded a small hill, and, there, spread out before me, were many springs and small pools of fresh, clear water. Round and about, there were all sorts of beautiful flowers and it was a most beautiful place.

"Malka mine, sweet Mimi, precious wife of mine, I present to you the site on which I shall erect your palace, and we shall live here and rule our domain together. Are you pleased with this, my belated wedding gift to you? This region is called the Springs of Banyas, and these waters do away with the digging of wells. In fact, I have plans to use hollowed-out halves of tree trunks to carry water right through our home. Tell me my love, if you approve of your new domicile."

For the first time in my life, I was speechless. Not a word, not a sound came from my throat. But I did fling myself at Nahyim and, squeezing as hard as I could, kissed him and stroked him, and showed him my approval. What a man. Truly, I was blessed. That night, we slept in our tent surrounded by the serenade of the Springs of Banyas. For me, it was a night to remember. I believe that Nahyim would also retain the memory of this night. In the morning, not far from the water, Nahyim began building our home. I later learned that he had paid someone, weeks before, in Jerusalem, to come here with a full caravan of dressed stones and rocks from the Judean hills, specifically for our home, and now he was laboring, building the walls. This was not to be a home of dried-mud bricks, but a sturdy and well-built home.

As I stood there gazing with adoration at my Nahyim at work, the voice spoke to me. "Mimi! Start walking. We have to talk."

"Oh, dear Ayl — don't tell me I have more work to do. Not now. Not when we're just getting started. If I have to leave Nahyim now or have to devote any more time to something else, I have a feeling I will be angry at you, and, then, I have another feeling that, if that happened — well I don't know really. Has anyone ever been angry at you? What is the penalty? Is it a bad thing? Oh, I just don't know. Please tell me."

"Hush now, Mimi, and give ear, for I have good news for you. That's why I summoned you to listen. I do not wish to wear you out with chore after chore. Neither do I wish that you be an unhappy person. You have been an obedient servant and have accomplished all that I have asked of you. It is time now for you to lead a normal life, and, so, here are my instructions for you. Here is where you will live long enough to raise your family, and see them settled. You will have children and bring them up here. You will teach them to walk in my ways. After they have established their own homes and destinies, you and Nahyim will leave this place — and vanish. I shall see to that. You will appear at an appropriate place, at an appropriate time, when I shall need you once more. Do you understand?"

"Do you mean to say that for years and years, Nahyim and I shall be here together and have a family and not be disturbed? Is that what I understand you to say ,Adoni?"

"Yes, Mimi — when I say something, I mean what I say. You did not misunderstand. Be fruitful and multiply, but understand that multiplication is a numeric process, and so we see that there are two people, a man and a woman. So, using that as a guide, we multiply two by two, or if you wish, two daughters and two sons, and we get an answer, which is four. I am not picky in that regard. That number is about right for a family during this period of history. The world is not, as yet, overcrowded. But, I do not want twenty children running all around you. This would give you no time to think, to learn, to do. You are not an animal but an intelligent human being, and I do not wish to see you having a flock but rather a manageable family — understood?"

"Oh, yes, yes. Very well understood. I shall be ready to get underway as soon as possible. You did say 'four,' didn't you?"

"That's right. Four. No More. And now it is time for me to be about my own work. I shall be guarding you at all times, and, if you need me for something important, please do not hesitate to call on me. I shall answer. Otherwise, I shall not bother you. Have a good time, and I shall see you, all being well — and I know that 'all being well' shall be the case — when the time comes. Now go back to Nahyim. I think he misses you. We have walked quite a way. Bye bye."

And just like that, I knew that our talk was over. I stood there while my mind chewed what I had just heard, and it tasted very good to me. I quickly returned to see and hear Nahyim rushing around crying "Mimi, Mimi," in a high-pitched voice.

I ran to him, and we embraced each other. He told me that he had looked up and did not see me, that he had been searching for me, and that dreadful thoughts of what had befallen me had run through his mind. I once more assured him that nothing dire would befall me for as long as I lived, for we were blessed by the protection of the Ruler of all the animals, the people, the earth, the sun and moon and stars, the wind, the water, everything that was, is, and shall be. He had nothing to fear. We were alive, we loved each other, and it was here that we would make our lives, together. I then told him of what had led me to take a walk — and of my instructions — and, when I finished, Nahyim just stood there and beamed as if his face were the sun.

"A family? Us? Children? Here? Now? Is that what you are saying Mimi? This is the place, and now is the time? Is that it?"

"Yup," said I. "The Lord wants us to create, and the order is four — yes four — children, gender unspecified; however, two plus two would be satisfactory. You are to be the father and I the mother. Is that all right with you, Nahyim?"

I shall not continue reporting the conversation. The rest of the afternoon and night is a personal matter, and no one else has need to know more.

A PLACE OF OUR OWN

For the first two weeks, Nahyim and Yofi dragged stones and rocks, and Nahyim continued to fit all the four walls together. He even had someone bring wooden pieces for placing over spaces for windows and a doorway. Every room had at least one window, and, when all the walls had been put together and sealed on the outside with black sticky stuff, there came the roof. I wondered what kind of covering would be on our roof, and I was amazed when I saw that Nahyim and his friend were placing wooden poles on the roof. Each of the poles was not more than a finger's width from the other. When I asked Nahyim what the poles were for, he said that he had planned on surprising me.

After a few days of this poling the roof, he stopped, and going to his supply of leather, started stitching. It took three more weeks of living in a tent before the stitching was finished, and I finally found out that this was to be our roof! He and his friend could not do it alone, so they sent for his friend's family and neighbors, and they came. They erected a ramp going up to the roof. The men with the biggest feet went onto the roof and spaced themselves next to each other. The rest of the men hauled the leather up the ramp, until the men on the roof could hold it, and then they started moving backward on the roof while the men on the ramp moved upward. In that way, they were able get this large blanket-like piece of leather onto the roof. As the first men on the roof reached the other end, they started rolling it like a rug, and the men from the ramp did likewise. The result was that this leather rug lay on the poles rolled up a bit on each end. Then the men stepped onto the roof-to-be, turned around, and unrolled the leather until it hung over each side of the house. We now had a roof, which had been oiled and shined, and when it rained, the rain would just run off the roof. Nahyim had made sure that there was plenty of leather left hanging on the front of the house, and had put two sturdy, tall cedar trunks into the ground and tied the leather to these poles, thus giving us a beautiful front area protected from the sun and rain. There were six rooms in our home. You entered into a large room through the front door and then a hallway straight ahead. Coming off this hallway were five rooms for sleeping or sitting. There was one room just past the front room that served as a kitchen or preparing and storing area for food. I would do my cooking outside in a smaller shed built for this purpose, but, on rainy days, I could do it under the front canopy, or the shed, as I pleased. To one side of the front, canopied area, there was a small stone hut which housed our bathroom. Later on, since we had to use the pools for bathing, my darling erected another small stone hut, specifically for my private bath. Half of the hut was on land and the other was in the water. With the leftover stones and rocks and another delivery of the same, Nahyim and his friend built a wall around our home grounds in order to establish that someone lived there. Then he erected a sign engraved in stone, which said Bayt Mimi uNahyim — the house of Mimi and Nahyim. Our home was complete.

We had a Chanukkat Habayit and invited our family, all our new friends, and all the neighbors we could find. I must admit we all had a wonderful time. Everyone brought food or wine. Someone brought a goat, another a few hens and a rooster, and someone even brought a pregnant ewe sheep and promised that the if the lamb were not a male, they would provide a ram for next season. The proper blessings were said, and the home was consecrated. Who would have thought that the Batya of Kinneret would grow up to be Mimi, the Mistress of this beautiful home? My heart thumped all day long. That night, my husband lay in our new bed (I had managed to put together a pallet for two, with a little help from my friends, and had sewn a down-filled bed for us. I was pleased that the first thing my husband did when he saw my present was to fall down on it and sleep. He was completely worn out by months of work, but he had finished before the rainy season. He slept through most of the next day, without waking, and arose sometime in the afternoon. I was busy stirring a pot of lentils, and he came up behind me, hugged me, and turned me around for a lovely kiss. He was awake. No doubt about it. I was happy for him as well as for myself. We ate, and I claimed a bit of weariness from the past day's doings, so I went to bed. He followed, and we both went into a deep and contented sleep later on.

TWO ARE BETTER THAN ONE

We had not lived for more than six months in our palace by the springs when I started to feel a bit unsettled in my stomach for a few mornings. I and soon discovered that I was with child. When I mentioned this to Nahyim, he jumped in the air, clapped his hands over his head, and was like a child with a new toy. I sat there smiling and let him get rid of his energy, but the joy did not leave his face for a moment. He settled down and talked, talked, talked about plans for the future child's room. His first worry was for a crib. His "professional opinion as an artisan" was that it should be made of aged olive wood and, instead of legs, should have curved rockers. He also wondered how big it should be. Should it be temporary — to be used for only a few months, until the baby was walking, or should it be larger in order to last for five to ten years. As he rattled on, I could only smile at his enthusiasm, pride, and joy. After having seen all types of males in my travels, I was sure that mine was the best of all, and he was mine. Oh, what a wonderful father he would be.

A few months later, when the belly kicking started, he would lay his hand or head on my stomach and smile as he felt the pounding from within my body. He would sit and watch, at times, the sudden jumps of my skin as a heel or hand, or something, pushed outward and made a sudden lump appear. Then, as time went by, we noticed that there were many of these sudden bumps, all jumping at the same time. That is when he started to worry that our forthcoming child had either too many arms or too many feet. This bothered him, and he told me of his concern. I told him not to worry. Had he forgotten that we were protected and that this was a blessing from on high? "Ahl Taydahg," ("don't worry") I told him. "Whatever will be born will be born and be a treasure to us, and an additional source of love. After all, this baby will be of both of us and will be just what you wanted. Now, stop this worrying, and rejoice in the coming event. Soon enough will it be, that you will get a little less sleep at night, so I would advise you to lie down, rest, relax and try to sleep away your worries and fears, because I have said so. See? I have no fears, and it is I who shall give birth. Calm yourself, before I have to worry about you!"

"Oh, Mimi. You are so right. Here I was thinking only of myself, my fears, my anxiety, and giving no thought to you. Forgive me, my love. I'll worry no more and leave all details of what is going on to the one who creates, either God or you, my adorable one. I cannot remember having lived without you. How did I ever manage, before we met? I'm the most fortunate man to have ever lived. Todah L'Ayl. (Thanks to God)."

After he finished this lovely speech, which I received most graciously, without interrupting him once, he took me in his arms, nuzzled his nose in my hair, and we kissed for a long time. I told him that we should have more talks like this — at least once a day. He smiled, and we went to sleep.

The birth was easy, and the pain which other women had described to me was not what I had expected. I only had to scream once, and finally it was over — and then it started again, and it was over even more quickly. I had given birth to a boy child, and I had also given birth to a girl child. The midwife handed the boy child to Nahyim, who was waiting in the front room, and that is when I gave birth to a daughter. I was exhausted and went to sleep; later, Nahyim related to me that his first thought was that there was only one crib and that he had been remiss in not foreseeing this double birth. There he was, with one child in each arm, while I slept, and did not know what to do. However, the midwife took charge and placed both babies in the crib, because there was plenty of room for them, and then told Nahyim to start working on another crib. She did this to get him out of the house, so that she could clean up and wake me after a while, to feed my children.

Oh, what a joy, what a pleasure it was just to hold them as they fed. To feel these beautiful little beings close to me, to count their forty fingers and toes, to see their eyes, trying to look at me and wonder what was going on. To think of them growing and walking and talking and — oh, the thoughts that strayed through my head! I uttered a prayer of thanks and fell asleep with both of them lying on me. The midwife then took them back to the cradle and rocked them to sleep. She stayed with us for three weeks, teaching me how to set up the household in order to care for the family in proper fashion.

I had decided, although she did not approve, to feed them whenever they cried for milk. If they cried — and were dry, I would feed them, and this seemed to work out fine. She told me that this might spoil them and that, later on, they would make other demands of me, but I answered that I did not think that children, at this age, knew what spoiling meant. When they were hungry, they were hungry, and, since I was their source of food, I must feed them. As it happened, the future proved me correct. But then, because Rav Hillel had taken great pains to ensure that I remembered his rule, how could I not be right? The son we named Gershon, and the daughter we named Gili.

For the first year, they were hardly able to express themselves, except to let me know they were wet and uncomfortable or needed milk. At two years they were toddling and babbling. Nahyim would often stare at them with wonder in his eyes, as if he were witnessing a continuing miracle. His delight with them knew no end, and, every time he passed me, he would give me a hug or a kiss and tell me how lucky he was. It is good to be appreciated, and, periodically, I returned the compliments. This was a period of wonder and discovery, as the children grew and as we grew as a family. Two years later, I gave birth to another set of twins, again a girl and a boy. The girl was first this time. We named them Shoshanah and Shimon.

Again, Nahyim was completely overjoyed with the birth of these two darlings, and Gershon and Gili were old enough to stare at the tiny babes and understand that these were their brother and sister. They accepted them at once, and there was no question that, from that moment, there was a bond between the four of them that could be seen, even by a stranger, and we knew that this was very rare and were glad of it. Again I thanked Ayl for my abundant riches, for I felt that no woman on earth had so much as I, and it made me joyful.

And so the years passed quickly, until there were no toddlers, until they were all almost grown and had attended a nearby village school. The sages had decreed that every city, every community, when established, must first set aside a cemetery for the community and then establish a school for the children. The reason for this was that one never knew when death would arrive, and children could not be expected to keep the law, unless they could read and understand it, so they had to learn — thus the need for a community school. All four of the children were excellent students and enjoyed learning. At the evening meal, the six of us would sit around the table and discuss the day's events, what was learned, what was accomplished, and then we would discuss the 'Law of the Day' and what it meant. Sometimes it was a heated debate, and sometimes there was agreement, but, between all of us, there was respect, kindness, and a willingness to listen. Hardly ever would there be a cross word uttered. Anger was not something in which any of us was interested. However, there were times, when the children came home, that they were upset by what had happened in school. Sometimes it was some child bullying another or the teacher reprimanding a child before the whole group. They saw, in these actions, that injustice was happening in front of their eyes, yet they did not know what to do. It was hard to advise them because we did not believe in disrespect to teachers or in getting into fights with other students. Yet, we could not allow them to think that they must be blind to injustice.

Finally, Nahyim and I told them that, if they thought that the teacher was being unjust or unfair, they should see the teacher after class, alone, and talk about the incident, saying that they had felt bad for the victim's embarrassment and asking what they could do. This would probably prompt an answer from the teacher, which might bode well for the future. Nahyim told them that, when bullying took place, the teacher should be told, and if nothing came of it and the bullying continued, they were to intervene by telling the bully to stop, because hurt was being committed, and this was wrong. Words were to be used, and, if the bullying stopped, all well and good. If the bullying did not stop, and since there were four of them together, they should all step between the bully and the victim and continue to ask the bully to stop. Since our two lads were tall for their age, and the sisters were as spunky as the brothers, they formed a formidable front, and they never had to do battle with anyone. At eighteen years of age, Gershon and Gili were married in a double wedding to two very nice mates, whom we had "chosen" for them after discussing their proposed choices. Nahyim and I never really figured out who it was that did the choosing, but every marriage had our blessing.

It was at the wedding that a guest from near Jerusalem told us that some of Yoshi's followers had claimed he was the King of the Jews and had been born to restore the rightful throne to Judea. The Roman ruler had personally questioned him and asked him if he really thought he was the King of the Jews. Yoshi had replied that since the Romans had brought the charge, it was no use arguing, and that he, Yoshi, knew that, no matter what he said, he would be found guilty. Yoshi had been executed, Roman style, slowly, just as had many hundreds and thousands of Jews, in previous years. These Romans were vicious, uncivilized pagans. But it was no use. Yoshi was dead, and I would never see his eager face again; so sad, such a good student and a good man. What a waste. Nahyim tried to console me, but I told him to give me time. I had to go through this myself. As I sat under the roof, outside the doorway, I asked myself why this had to be.

Could not the road taken have curved in another direction? Was this destined? Then I remembered the story of Job and thought to myself that each person must repeat that story, in some way, whenever the death of a close one takes place, or in the case of some other great loss. I thought too, of my Ima and my brothers, who must have mourned my disappearing, never seeing me again. Did they sit "Shivah" (mourning), or what? Did they think I had been murdered? I did not know. At that moment, the voice came.

"Mimi, when I told you that I would see to your needs, I also took care of your mother. Someone who had traveled reported sighting you and reported on what had been said about you. They knew that you were alive, well, and were carrying out your mission. As long as they lived, news of you drifted to them and comforted them. As for the present, I, too, am sorry for the loss of Yoshua. I had great hopes for him, and he was cut down too young and could not accomplish his mission in his lifetime. You see, some of his followers made bad decisions. The King made bad decisions. From these decisions, suffering has arisen. Do not go to Jerusalem — neither you nor your loved ones — for a decision has been made by the Romans to destroy the city completely. I will protect a remnant of the people and, especially, you and your close ones. No harm will come to you or them. But I fear for many of Jacob's children. But, as it was with Babylon, so shall it be with Rome. One day, you shall see the land spring up with the sounds of the Torah being read, my people dancing in the streets, and the joyous sound of freedom from oppression. It will take a long time for them to go through the crucible. After Egypt, Moses and my people, wandered for forty years until they reached this land. Now they will have to wander for many more than hundreds of years before returning —but this you may be sure of — they will return. But no more of this. I shall not need your services for quite a while. Enjoy your grandchildren, see to their proper training, and, when the time comes, you and Nahyim will leave this place and go to a location which I will tell you, and, there, you will sleep, until once more you will go to work. Have a good life in this existence. I shall take care of your health and ensure that your skin does not wrinkle. Be assured of that. Nahyim shall also not lose his vigor. Don't worry. Be happy. L'hitra-ot."

And that was that. My schedule had been set for me. I was sorry about the destruction of Jerusalem and the suffering of the people, but I knew that I could do nothing about it. I felt so helpless. When I told Nahtahn all of this, he threw his arms around me, held me tight, and said softly,

"Mimi, my Motik, don't despair. You are not a god. You are a messenger. We do not understand all the ways of nature. How can we understand all the complicated ways of humans, families, cities, and nations? All we can do is that which we know will not harm or hurt. It is only by doing that we can earn the right to look at ourselves without shame, for that is what makes us different from the jackal. Do you not think that our Creator also mourns when people act in a mean, hostile fashion, or lie, or steal? But that is what free will is all about. Don't you remember our discussions? Come now, if we cannot make the world into a Gan Eden right now, then, at least let us make a small garden of joy and light here and now. Maybe that light will spread a little farther and empower others to do good. Have faith, Mimi — not only in Ayl, but also in ourselves, for we have the tools with which to make this change happen, even if only in a small way. "

I looked up at my wonderful, wise, and lovable man, kissed him, and told him of my love for him. He had, with his words, wiped away much of the grief which had tortured me. Life was, once again, beginning to feel good. Later, he made me feel better.

A few years later, the younger twins had a double wedding in the same manner. We had all been blessed, and now Nahyim and I had the house to ourselves. It was much quieter than ever before, and we missed having our children with us, but we sometimes did spend Shabbat together, for the children, and later, the grandchildren enjoyed bathing in the pools and springs. The time went quickly, as it does when life is pleasant, and when the youngest grandchild had reached 13 years of age and had become a responsible person, I knew that the time was short and that a voice would call me. Thinking back over my lives, I could see that being chosen had its joys and responsibilities and yet also had moments of sadness, for I knew that Nahyim and I would have to depart from our family, from our home, and from our time. When I was a child, growing up, I had had a vision of a long life, family, joy and sadness — but never of a life of leaving, and leaving, and leaving. My heart was heavy, and I could see that these thoughts were also with Nahyim. Finally I opened the subject, and he admitted to the same feelings yet knew that what must be must be accepted, and we slept. Then the time came. As I was returning from my morning bathing, the voice came, and I stood as a statue when I heard it.

DESPAIR AND RETROSPECT

The voice told me to go to our home, prepare, and, at the end of the day, bid each other a pleasant sleep, and when we awakened, we would be elsewhere, but not far. We did as we were directed and slept.

Upon awakening, we were in a tent at the shore of Kinneret but closer to the town, called Tiberius. After breakfast, walking along the shore, the voice came and spoke.

"Mimi, there is an academy here where great sages gather. Go in and tell them that there will be no prayers at the Temple Mount for countless centuries to come. Also, tell them that this decree was written because of many tragic choices by many people. The fault lies not only with the Children of Jacob, but also with those who do not understand the meaning of the Law and who try to invent dreams out of the reality with which humans must deal. Tell the sages to counsel the people to accept this tragedy, to learn the lessons of history, continue to study the world, and try to live in peace, while living under the rule of a stranger, while remembering who they are, for they are a destined people, a conscience to the world, and the descendants of kings, prophets, and priests, both royal and holy. There are stirrings around Jerusalem, and there are people who would rebel against Rome. Counsel the sages to tell the people that this cannot be. Should they rise, blood will fertilize the fields, and only a remnant of the many shall remain. Go now. Tell them, for the time is short."

I heard, and I obeyed. Nahyim and I rode into T'veria and found it to be the same, quiet, small fishing town which we had visited on our former trip. Entering the town, we enquired of a passing woman, and were directed to the Bet Rabbim (the house of the sages). I entered. As I walked in, I saw them sitting around a massive table, which was covered with many scrolls. They looked up and noticed me.

"Yes, daughter. What can we do for you? What is it you need?"

"Nay, Adoni," said I, "I have no needs, for my needs are completely seen to. I have been sent to convey a message to you. Ayl Elyon has sent me to tell you of your responsibility for now. Please listen to me, for there is not much time."

As I expected, there was one or more of those present who did not like a woman telling them anything. One of them somewhat younger than the others rose and spoke.

"Dear girl, do you really think we have time to listen to a woman's ravings? Tell your dreams to someone else. We have important work to do. Can you not see that we are working with the Law? Do you not understand what that means? How dare you interrupt such an important undertaking?"

Before I could speak, the young man started to shake and shiver. He seemed to be completely out of control of his body. He tried to speak, but all one could hear were squeaks and mouthings but nothing that could be understood. I felt sorry for the poor scholar, because he could not know — or could not understand — and I rushed toward him and enfolded him in my arms, saying, "Ayl, please stop this. He didn't know."

The shaking stopped. The man sat down. I continued.

"As you can see, I speak the truth. I come as a messenger and not as a bother. I wish no trouble but only to convey the message which I have been told to convey to you only. What you choose to do shall determine the lives of many of our people."

I finished telling them what had to be done, turned around, and left, accompanied by the sound of silence.

Weeks later, as we wandered, we heard that the people had not heeded the word of the Lord and had rebelled against the Romans and defeated the Legion which had been stationed in the area. Not only that, but they had established a new Kingdom of Israel in the Town and region of Betar, which was less than a day's journey from Jerusalem. There, they were minting money, raising more of an army, and bidding all the remaining Judeans to come to Betar for their own safety. Their leader or king was called Shimon bar Kosba. He was also the leader of the troops. It appears that the Roman rulers decided that this second rebellion (the first one had been stamped out at Masada many years ago) would be the last and sent many troops and their best general to wipe out this hornet's nest. They completely surrounded the area of the rebellion and literally starved the people. When the defenders were weak, the Romans moved their legions in and killed everyone, man, woman, and child. No one was left. The fields and streams ran red with the blood of one-half million or more people. And later I heard that a certain sage, named Akiba, had called the pretender to the throne of David "the Star of David" — Bar Kochba. This kingdom lasted only a few years.

Oh, what a fool. This Rabbi Akiba person was captured by the Romans and put to death with dreadful tortures. But, this Rav Akiba had also had a list of great accomplishments in his lifetime. He organized academies, taught people how to study and interpret the law and how to start codifying the law; he seemed to be a good organizer. However, I, for one, never forgave him for not stopping this tragic insurrection. Oh, well. People make choices, sometimes good, sometimes bad, and sometimes horrible.

We returned to our retreat and, saddened by the events which had befallen our land and people even as we watched, we knew that Ayl would not desert us, and that the children of Jacob would someday return to their ancestral home. We slept and did not waken for almost two hundred years.

I DO NOT MEET CONSTANTINE

We awoke to find ourselves far from Judea. We also found ourselves surrounded by a new language, that of the Romans. It was quite astonishing to us, when we found ourselves able to converse quite easily in this language, although we had not learned it previously, except for a few words we had heard from soldiers. We found ourselves in our tent, on the shores of a large body of water and were told, later, that this body of water separated two parts of the same land, and that Tyre, Jerusalem, and other places we were accustomed to lay to the south and east, many weeks of caravan travel. I wondered why Ayl had placed us here, next to a very large city, which was named for the Emperor Constantine. Our needs had been taken care of quite well, and we found provisions within the tent after we had awakened. When we stepped out of the tent, we found that the water was close by and bathed ourselves. God knows how many years we had gone without washing up. We struck up conversations with passing people and found out that we had slept for about two centuries and that Constantine had named this city after himself. What is more amazing is that his mother, Helena, had not been a pagan but had some strange idea that our Yoshi had been some sort of a demi-god or something like that. At that time, I did not completely understand the situation. It appears that my admonitions had somehow gone unheeded. Some of Yoshi's followers had named him as the Messiah, and, after he had died, it was told that a small group of his women followers, in a fit of mourning had visualized him as being alive. There was bitter fighting going on between his followers — some saying that he was the Messiah, promised by other people; some said he was God; some said he was none of these and that he was a modern-day prophet and others kept their peace. Constantine, knowing that his mother did not worship the gods of Rome, declared that, throughout the empire, all religions would be tolerated. The slaughter of Jews, Jesus's followers, and other humans ceased, and instead of coliseums, hippodromes were built in order that horse and chariot races could take place. For a while, it seems there was a quiet period, when families could be together, and there was a Pax Romana for God's remnant folk. (Roman Peace).

When we arrived in Constantinople, there were all kinds of rumors. It was said that, although she was getting on in years, Helena, Constantine's mother, was the true power behind the throne. Others said that Constantine was a pagan, but the ones who claimed this were full of sour grapes. That's what Nahyim suggested to me.

After we had settled in, the voice spoke once again, saying, "Time to go to work, Mimi. You are to arrange a meeting with the Queen and counsel her to advise her son not to allow any religion to have any authority in the government. The two must be kept separate, because humans have been using government religions to control the people and interfere with the true function of a belief in me and in my laws. It is apparent that this system does not work for the benefit of the people. In fact, every time priests are involved in religion, more corruption is evident. The two have totally different uses and should not be mixed in good governance. Now, I know that you may be a bit shy in saying all of this, but don't worry. I shall be with you, and, should you falter, the words will come, and the message will be delivered. Now, you and Nahyim go to the palace, and advise them that an important messenger shall arrive tomorrow and has a message for Queen Helena. Understood?"

What could I do? I assented and immediately told Nahyim, and we left for the Palace. When we arrived, of course, there was an armed guard. We waited while the guard told his superior, and, I suppose, the message was transmitted up the line until it reached the Queen. This took one-half of the day. It was really tiresome, just waiting and waiting. Finally the word arrived that we had been granted an audience and were to join her for the mid-day meal on the morrow.

We had the rest of the day and went sightseeing. There were many new buildings, and the waterfront was very busy with boats bringing in all kinds of supplies for the new seat of government and for all the houses needed for the growing population. We could hear many languages being spoken, although Roman seemed to be most common. We noticed that there were two kinds of people who were native to this land. There were some fair-skinned people, some of them even with red or light colored hair, and some people who were of darker complexion with dark hair, some curly, some straight. We questioned a street vendor, and he explained that this land was a crossroad for east and west and north. There were people from the north and some from the west who typified the light-haired groups, and the people from the south and east were darker in skin and hair. That was his opinion. Nahyim ventured that it might have something to do with the heat of the sun. He explained that a green leaf, plucked from a tree and left in the sunlight, would soon turn brown. That seemed to make sense, although I was sure that it was more complicated than that, but did not wish to argue with my adorable playmate.

We found an inn which met our needs, and, ensuring that our beasts were comfortable and adequately furnished with food and water, we supped and slept. The following day, we appeared at the Palace at the appointed time and patiently waited while our arrival was announced and permission to enter was granted. We were met by an armed guard who escorted us for what seemed too long a time, through various corridors and arches, until we arrived at the Queen's quarters. He left, and we were escorted into an antechamber, where we were seated to await the Queen's presence. We were told that we should approach her no more than an arm's length, bow from the waist, and speak only after she had greeted us. A few moments later, another door opened, and the Queen entered, accompanied by two attending women. We stood, bowed at the waist, and waited.

"Good day to both of you. What is this message of great import which has been addressed to me? But first, tell me your names and where you are from."

"My name is Mimi, and this is my dear husband Nahyim. We are both from what we children of Jacob call our Holy Land. I know that it has been renamed; however we still remember it as the land of our ancestors."

"I see," she said, "Well, I am Queen Helena, and, since you are my guests, please follow me, and we shall eat and talk. I have many questions to ask."

We followed and arrived at a room, which had a table large enough for at least fourteen guests, and padded chairs, cleverly constructed, so that when a wooden pin was removed from the sides, the chair back could be lowered to form a couch. What a nice idea, I thought. One does not have to move after eating one's fill, but can lie there and nap.

It would also be just the thing for the Passover meal, for we are bidden to eat while reclining, in order to remind ourselves that we were not slaves.

Then I sighed and thought of the old days when Nahyim and I used to picnic at the shore of the sea, or near a pond. Ah, to relive those days again. Although I had enjoyed them, I did not really appreciate them until now. Then I wondered why we cannot really appreciate what we have until we no longer have it. But my thoughts were interrupted by the voice of the Queen and her question.

"Tell me, Mimi, what is the Holy Land like? Is there truly milk and honey, as it is written?"

I was immediately taken aback by this question. What did this Roman woman know of our Torah? How had she come across this description from our past? I did not know her well enough to pry and examine her, so I just answered the question as best I could.

"Well, that is difficult to answer, but I shall try. The Holy City is in ruins. When the final battle was over after the rebellion, the Roman army razed it and burnt it until all that remains is mostly a pile of rubble on the top of the Mount, and the upper and lower cities are also in ruins. The countryside is ravaged, and there are very few of our people left in the whole region. Most of them have been killed. The remainder appear to be spread throughout the empire. Many of them are in Rome, some free, some in the army, and some as slaves. We have not, as yet, encountered any of them here in your great city. Where there were once towns and crops, nothing grows, for the earth was salted before the conquerors left. There are some regions where strangers had been brought in by the Romans to establish trading posts, inns for merchants and traders, and a small garrison in some places. The millions of our kinsmen who once lived in our sweet land, are no longer seen. Yet, those who survive look forward to their return, for their faith in the Covenant remains firm. Practically speaking, though, there is not much to see there, except for ruins."

"Oh, how wistful and sad your words are, Mimi. Is it not terrible how men make war and destroy, rather than live in harmony and build?"

This declaration coming from this Roman woman absolutely stunned us. Nahyim looked at me and seemed to be having the same thoughts as I.

He spoke to her. "Excuse me, Queen Helena. I noticed before that you had spoken of milk and honey. Now you speak as did one of our prophets of long ago. How did you come by these thoughts, these ideas, and these ideals? If you will excuse my saying so, we never expected utterances such as these to come from any person from Rome, let alone royalty."

"Ah, Nahyim, you do not know our history very well. Do you not remember what a good friend to the Jews Julius Caesar was? He admired their family loyalty, and their study of the law. Of all the peoples he had ruled, he admired the Judeans as exemplars. Also, did you not know there were wives of Emperors of Rome who had become members of your faith? Remember that your people, since the time of Solomon, established trading posts all over the world, and took with them their history and their faith. In some places, your god is well known. I myself have questioned learned members of your people and have adopted many of their ideas. The concept of one Creator, one god, appeals to me as being the most sensible explanation for many questions dealing with the nature of the world and humans. There is still much I do not understand, but I assure you that I am not an enemy of your god. I am puzzled by the many writings of those who are called prophets. They seem to be very bitter people and, for the most part, are always speaking of punishment, as if God were lurking, just waiting for a chance to catch people transgressing the law, and meting out harsh punishment. Yet, there was this Jesus person, whom the Judeans called Yoshua, who seemed to offer a kinder interpretation of the law and of a kinder God. All this is very confusing, don't you think? Have you heard of him? It appears that there are many, many different opinions about what he said, who he was, and what he did. Do you know of him?"

Nahyim answered this question for us. "Yes, dear Queen, we certainly have. But have you heard of the man from whom he took much of his ethical and moral principles? The man was called Hillel and was deemed the greatest sage of his time by many of the people. His writings and teachings were available to Yoshua, and, when he was teaching his crowds, Yoshua would quote from Hillel constantly. You see, this Jesus, as you call him, was a man who saw quite clearly the results of the Hellenization of many of our people, and it troubled him, because they were forgetting the behavioral code of our Law, that which we call Torah. He did not like that the Priests were shirking their duties, and that the wealthy were not seeing to the poor. The Jubilee of the land was being forgotten, and many families lost their homes which had been in the family for more than nine hundred years. He spoke of making a better world, where people would realize that kindness was good for everyone and that justice was for all."

"Really? I had not realized that Yoshua and Hillel were such philosophers. But what is this that I hear about argumentation and differences among your people about this man, Yoshua? It appears that many people have differing opinions about him. I do not understand why he has caused such bitterness among your people."

While I was listening to Nahyim and to the Queen, I silently tried to summon Ayl, for I knew that I would have to say something, and that I really didn't know if I could make sense. I felt a calmness come over me and knew that everything would be all right, for the Lord was literally with me. So I smiled and spoke.

"If I may, your Highness, I should like to explain. I assume that you have servants. Some of them serve you with a smile and willingly, and when they are through serving, you are completely satisfied and thank them. There are other servants who serve you, albeit without any smile and with a grudging attitude. When they speak of you to their friends, they may pick and choose their words to describe you in such a manner that would mirror what they are, in terms of who they are, deep inside. It is probable that all who have heard of Yoshua may pick and choose from that which they hear, according to their own desires and inclinations. Their choice might be based on what is, or what they wish it to be. And so, those who followed him told tales according to their own eyes and ears, each person having heard only that which was important to that person. In this way, someone can be described in many ways, according to how people see that person. Yoshua said many things, and those who followed him in time remembered only that which they wanted to hear, and, if they heard something that they might not have agreed with, over time, their memory might have lessened, and their imagination might have changed what was in the past. Why, did you know that there is a group, which says that Yoshua was a god? How he would have laughed at that. There are others who claim he was a son of god. How ridiculous. If a god is a true god, can he not create a son without having to go through a nine-month waiting period with a woman? Miriam, his mother, never claimed that Ayl was the father. Neither did Yoshua. He did say that we were all children of Ayl, every mortal being, and that we were to be judged by that which we do. In that sense, I guess, Yoshua was also a child of Ayl. There are others who make stories up about how he died. Truth to tell, it was Romans who killed him like a common criminal, because some of his stupid followers had called him their King. Rome could not stand for that. So they killed him. Dear Queen, there is just too much violence, and this violence bodes ill for the people of the Empire. I beg you, speak to the Emperor and ask him to accept the doctrine of peace to all men, goodwill, and, as Hillel said 'Do not do unto others that which is hateful to you. That is the law. All else is commentary.' Please ask him to ensure tranquility for all peoples."

The Queen sat quietly. For a long time, she did not move but seemed to stare into somewhere beyond, far away. Then she spoke, saying, "I shall speak to Constantine. I do not know whether it will be of any use, since we have had news that we are about to be attacked and must go to war. However, tonight at dinner, I shall have a word with him. This saying of Hillel has impressed me so much that I have decided that, at the first opportunity, I shall travel to your land for a visit to the places where Hillel was and to see what there is left of your Holy City. Meanwhile, I shall question others of this Jesus to find out how many different opinions there are. I do believe you when you say that we are all children of the same Creator. I came to that realization a while back. But I do not know what I can accomplish with this knowledge."

I looked at her, feeling very sorry for this lovely woman with such a burden. Being a queen is hardly a lifetime picnic, and I saw how worried she was. So I tried to reassure her.

"Oh, dear Queen Helena, please know that our God is with those who choose rightly. I can see that you are a most virtuous person, with high regard for the people. Take a lesson from my people. We tried governing ourselves with the Laws of God. It did not work out so well because people made bad choices, and the prophets who chastised the people did not have too much effect on them. Government, using God as a shield, became corrupt and cruel. The law of God governs behavior toward one another. God is the judge of that behavior.

"Government rules over all human endeavor, and should always be looking for the best solutions for all the inhabitants. Heretofore, it has been those with property and wealth who have profited from that system because it was those people who ruled. The government must be for all, and justice must be for all. It might be best to keep religion as far away from government as possible, since it has been perverted to the point where no one — no one — knows what the words mean. The law of kindness and love of the Creator's world must be uppermost. As Hillel said, 'All else is commentary.' But I see the afternoon grows late, and we have a journey ahead of us. May we be excused?"

She again said nothing and seemed to be somewhere else. "Yes, I suppose we must part, since the afternoon latens. Oh, how I wish you two could abide here, so that we could converse more. But, I would not wish to impose on you. If you ever wish to visit again, please do not hesitate. You are always welcome." She picked up a stick and tapped a metal bell, twice. Immediately two servants appeared and bowed. She addressed them softly, "Please escort my guests out, and, as you pass my kitchen, tell the cooks to provide them with food and drink for a long trip. Also, see that each is provided with one of the guest packets of gold coins. See that it is done. As for you, Mimi and Nahyim, Ave, and may your journey be easy and your god be with you in all you do."

We bowed and backed out the door to follow the two servants and, later, exited the palace laden with food, drink and gold. My goodness! Never had I been treated so royally. Well, what do you expect, coming from a queen of an empire? We returned to our inn, just as the sun had set. We checked on our donkeys and fed and watered them, and bade them goodnight. We went to our room, stored our food and drink, and went to the dining area, where dinner was being placed on the tables. After eating, we went for a short walk and back to our room. Later on, we went to sleep, quite contented.

We Can Do No More

Dear, dear. We just heard that there had been arguments between certain groups of followers of Yoshua and that Constantine, after a great battle, called a meeting of the heads of the sect in a place called Nicaea.

They have completely ruined Yoshua's reputation, and I fear that their pronouncements will bode ill for the world. Nahyim and I were on our way back to Banyas, to see if our home was still there, and to take a vacation. We traveled slowly, since we had no messages to deliver and wished to see the countryside. Yofi also enjoyed the slow pace and frequent stopping. One day, we were overtaken by a group of merchants who were heading in our direction, and they told us all the news from the empire. Nahyim and I looked at each other and just shook our heads. We had done that which we could. I wish we could have done more. But, Ayl had often said that all humanity had been born with the gift of making choices and that sometimes we messengers were sent. It was up to people to listen and learn, or choose to ignore.

We finally arrived at Banyas, and were astounded that there were more homes there, and that our own house stood empty and clean. It seems that most of the people living in the area were our descendants. We did not tell them exactly who we were but did convince them that we were also descended from the people who had lived in this home, and so they allowed us to live in the house, which Nahyim had built for us. Yofi, of course, was delighted because he also knew that he could rest, relax, and enjoy the pool and scenery. One night, I turned to Nahyim and asked him, "Sweetie, what would happen if we had more children?

Would that not be hilarious? What would be the relationship of these children to these descendants of ours? It had been many years since we have last been here and our own children have long ago slept with our ancestors."

Nahyim drew a diagram on the ground, with arrows pointing at each person, and showed a direct line from us to the four children, and then, lines spreading out. Then, instead of names, he drew two circles farther out with lines going up to us. If we were to have more children, their brothers and sisters would have died years ago. But, he said that we had better await word from Ayl, for we might still have work to do. I sighed and saw the wisdom of his words.

The days and weeks passed, and I saw that I could become easily accustomed to living like this for a long, long, time. It was so pleasant to go out in the morning and watch children splashing in the waters and hear their voices chirping and laughing. There is nothing in the world like the laughter of children. But, just as I thought that Ayl might have forgotten us, the voice came, the same as always, soft and still.

"Shalom, Mimi. Have you had a good rest? Are you ready for another trip? There is some work to be done. I need you to go somewhere. You probably will not be back here for a very long time, so look around and enjoy the rest of the day. Get a good night's sleep, for, on the morrow, when you awaken, you will be somewhere else. Again, we shall try some tutoring. Maybe, this time, it will work. Do not worry about provisions and such. It is all taken care of.

We shall talk more in the morning about your task. Sleep tight. I'll see to that." And with that, the voice was gone.

I went to tell Nahyim, who was sitting outside watching the children, and, when I started to relay the message to him, he said, "A funny thing happened this time, Mimi mine. I, too, heard the voice and recognized that I must attend to the words. We have another mission and, so, have to say goodbye to this peace and rest. I wonder where and when we shall be tomorrow. I still can't get used to going to sleep one time, and arising years later, yet aware of language. Our Creator moves in mysterious ways. It is truly amazing."

"And, Nahyim, look at all we remember and all we have learned. We can speak many languages. We understand some of the happenings of history. We have known Ayl, and yet still live. Would you have it any other way? The best thing is that we have had all of this and have also had each other. Who would not wish to live our lives?

"You're absolutely right Mohtik (sweetness). We are like the soil and the trees, perfect together. But, sometimes, I wonder what it might have been like if we had met, married, and settled down without your mission. Of course, by now, we would have been long gone, but I just cannot help wondering what might have been."

"Oh, come now, Nanu! You got married. We had four children, and we brought them up to be fine human beings. We watched them marry and have our grandchildren, and yet we can sit here and still remember it all. Is it not preferable to what might have been? Ayl has granted us extra life, not only for the mission's purpose but also so that we may enjoy our time together stretched out farther and farther, without diminishing our love. Have I not been a satisfactory mate? Have I not been attentive to your needs? I know that you have been the only man I could ever love, for you have seen to my needs and been an attentive and loving husband."

"Mimi, I shall be silent. You have been the only woman in my existence who has made me glad to have been born. Every day with you brings new joy, more love — and if only I could sing, I would sing your praises to the world. Unfortunately, my art is centered on the crafting of leather and that does not equate to instant musical talent. You know, sometimes when you do not see me, I watch you in wonder, thanking Ayl for our meeting. I cannot think of life without you. I still see you as I did the first day, so long ago, when I bethought myself bewitched by the sudden beauty of the world. I still think of that time whenever I see you. You are not only beautiful of face and form, but you have a mind which lends itself to all kinds of conversation, and your sense of humor and of the ridiculous never fails to amuse me. If all the people of this earth were as intelligent as my wife, men would not go off to war, not wishing to leave their homes and their mates. Ah, Mimi, I love you more each day."

"Well! That is a statement of reassurance, which would be quite acceptable to any woman. Your homage, sir, is accepted, and you may approach your princess for a royal hug and kiss."
And so it went for the rest of the day, and, at nightfall, we slept well.

SIT DOWN AND SAND UP (NOT A MISPRINT)

The next morning, when we awoke, the weather was uncomfortably warm. We were lying on a plush rug, upon which a comfortable double pad was situated. There was a large tray on another rug, which was replete with a healthy meal and drink. Near the entrance to the tent was a sack, which we discovered was full of grain for our donkeys. Outside the entrance, there was a well, bucket and rope, and a clay basin. We filled the basin with water, and the animals thanked us kindly, and we set out the food for them. Then we went in to eat. While we had been outside, we saw a strange town in the distance and noted that much of the surrounding soil seemed to be sand hills, such as may be seen in many places, either by the sea or inland where there is no rain. We knew not where we were. Later, we enquired of a passing caravan, and they told us that the nearby town was called Yatrib and was a hub for traders. We found out that the population had among it a large number of our fellow religionists, whose ancestors had arrived here in King Solomon's times, when he had established trading posts along the spice and silk routes.

There were two or three very powerful Jewish clans here, and they exerted much influence in the city. We took a short trip from our tent to the city gates, and, when we entered, we found that we had entered by the caravan gate. There was a huge square, and half of it was devoted to animals, which were kept behind a fence. Around this corral were inns called imarets, where the traders ate and slept. We toured all day long, meeting with some of our long-lost kinsmen and being welcomed by them. They told us that they would send some people out to help us pack the tent and belongings and bring them into the city, for it was dangerous to sleep in the wilderness. There was no law in the desert, and small groups were plundered as a matter of course, by roving pagans, who thought that their heritage was to collect loot.

Later in the day they did send some young men with camels, to help us. The men were very efficient, and, soon, all of our worldly goods were being hauled into the city, by these slow load carriers who could walk on the sand as if they were walking on grass, such was their grace. When we arrived we found ourselves welcomed into a spacious home, belonging to a member of the Khybar clan. They immediately showed us to a well-appointed guest room in the house and ensured that our animals were fed and watered and safely secured with their livestock. At this point, I had almost given up on Ayl. I did not know why we were in this place or what we were supposed to do. But, based on past experience, I knew that the voice would tell me when the time came. I decided to enjoy myself before my mission started.

That evening, after we had settled in our comfortable room, we were invited to a feast. When we arrived out of doors, there were rugs all over the sand, and there were women stirring pots over fires, while men were turning spits with giant pieces of meat being prepared. As we walked out the door, we heard shouts of "Salaam Aleikem, Salaam!."

We looked around and found that we were the center of interest. The feast was in our honor, welcoming us. It felt so good hearing familiar words in this strange place. We seated ourselves and were immediately served with fruits and vegetables and meats and lentils, and, oh — I cannot describe all the food. There were also drinks of all sorts, including the juice of the vine, which is called Yahyin. It tasted so good, but after a while, I felt a little dizzy and drank only water. There were musicians among them who played many instruments, banging, tinkling, and blowing, and small handheld harps, and the women started dancing; the men clapped, and it was delightful.

As the night latened, a clamor was heard from outside the wall, and when the gate was opened someone announced that there had been trouble in the town of Mecca. A man was being hunted, and he had asked asylum. At once, the men sprang into action. They assented to grant refuge to this man, and, taking no chances, they armed themselves and joined others to guard the town from other strangers. As luck would have it, he was brought to the house where we were staying, and he was fed and given a room to sleep. He was very tired and so they did not even bother to question him about the events leading up to his arrival. When it was clear that there would be no fighting, everyone went to their quarters, except for some of the young men who had volunteered to patrol the outside of the town to ensure night safety. After Nahyim and I thanked our hosts, we all said "Good night" and prepared for sleep. Then, it happened —

"Good evening, Mimi and Nahyim. I trust you enjoyed yourselves here in Yatrib. But I must interrupt your gaiety with your next job. Again, you will counsel an important person. Again you will present him with a choice. How he chooses will be up to him, but at least you may be able to influence him. You know about the lessons in public speaking and all of that, so I will not repeat. However, he has come into contact with some descendants of the pagan followers of Yoshua and they have tried to convince him of their 'three parts of God' theory. I shall not bother to explain, but I shall make it clear that I am not three parts. I have no parts. I have no body. I am the Creator, and I am One. Make him see this, for it is of vital importance that he does. One day, his followers will conquer much of this part of the earth, and I do not want him to teach them fairy tales, for they already have their own — a goddess of the moon, spirits called djinns hiding in every rock or cave, or tree, ready to pounce. Idiots, I tell you. But that is not your problem.

You are to advise him on the proper attitude toward the creator of the heavens and the earth and everything contained therein. In the morning, engage him in conversation, and he will welcome the chance to learn. What he does with that learning will be up to him. I am glad that you have been welcomed here, for I knew that this clan still remembers Abraham and his practice of welcoming all guests. He and Sarai would have been proud of these descendants of theirs. I leave you now. Tomorrow, you start your work. I want both of you to work with this young man. Sleep well."

And we did.

Who Said WHAT????

At breakfast the next day, we met the young man. He appeared to be somewhere in his late 20s or early 30s. It didn't matter. Nahyim sat next to him and mentioned that we were very interested in him and his story and asked if he would like to meet with us outside, somewhere in the shade. He assented, and we three strolled out together. We brought one of our thick rugs; and I carried a jug of water, and we settled under a shady tree.

Nahyim spoke first. "Mehmet, you already know my name, Nahyim. This is my wife Mimi. We would like to exchange stories with you so that we may all learn from each other. What say you?

Without hesitation, Mehmet spoke up, saying, "I am happy to meet you, Mimi. It is good to make new friends. Of course, we can tell each other of our lives, and I have found that all new friends have had experiences which can teach others who have not lived similar lives. We may all learn something new this way."

So, he began his narrative telling of his childhood, his travels as a caravan master for his future wife. He also told of his meeting with all kinds of people who had discussed their ideas of gods and life and how he had had strange experiences of suddenly falling asleep and seeing visions, or hearing voices. He spoke of his hearing of stories of Abraham and his descendants and of the slavery in Egypt and the flight into the wasteland, and of Moses the giver of the law. He also spoke of his meeting with people who told him that Yoshua had been the son of God, and others who had told him that Yoshua had been a god himself. Mehmet was quite confused as to the truth of all these stories, but said that he had come to the conclusion that if there was one creator, as the Bible of the Jews stated, then it would follow that God was only one. And there could be no other. He told us that when he tried to speak in Mecca about this, the priests who were in charge of the Kaaba, the big black stone which was worshiped as a pagan shrine, were enraged at him, because they felt he was attacking their livelihood, and that they had chased him the day before, in order to separate his head from his body. He opined that this was an unhealthy situation for his well-being.

He did not approve of that, and we agreed that it was, indeed, a very unhealthy spot to be in, and that keeping one's head is necessary to living a good life. He looked worried. So I spoke to him thusly,

"Fear not, Mehmet. Nahyim and I have been sent by the One God in order to comfort you and to tell you that your enemies shall not prevail. There will come a day when the Kaaba shall be the place where people from all over the earth shall come and worship that One Creator. But, be warned. This is what you must do. You must write down your message for the people, so that they know your exact words and when you said them. This is most important, because if you do not, those who come after you are gone will twist what you have said to meet their own needs. It has happened before to other great leaders, so beware."

"But, Nahyim, Mimi, I cannot do that, for I do not know the art of reading and writing. Although I have tried, I cannot master the skill of producing words from the marks which my eyes see on the scrolls. All I can do is speak what I know and feel. What can I do?"

Nahyim answered, "You must get yourself a scribe who will write down every word you utter when you speak to the people. In fact, it would be better to have three scribes doing this. After you have finished speaking, they must read, to each other and to you, what they have written down, and then everyone must agree to what was actually said. Then the three scribes must each copy down the true words and save them, in the case where there might be a question of what you had really said. This is the only way true witness can be made of your words."

I then added, "Yes, Mehmet. Nahyim's words are wise. And while we are discussing your words, I have been told to show you how to make sure that your words are heard and understood by all. I shall now give you some rules to follow. These are fairly easy to follow and need only a little practice. The first rule is, that when you are speaking to a large group, speak slowly, for it is difficult to understand fast speech in a crowded place. The second rule is to pronounce each word clearly and distinctly, so that each word is heard without being misunderstood. The third rule is to pick out one person in the crowd and look only at that one person, as if you are speaking only to him or her. That way, your voice will take on a personal touch and enable each member of the crowd to believe that you are speaking only to him or her. Those are the rules of speech making which you should learn and follow. As for what you say — you should start by telling the crowd what you are going to teach them, then you should teach them, and lastly your should tell them what you taught them. This is to ensure that they will follow your thoughts and, in the end, remember that which you have said. That is all I have to tell you about teaching and speaking to large groups. I would also like to speak to you of that which the Creator wishes for human beings to do on this earth. I shall speak of this only if you wish to hear it."

"You two seem to be truth-speaking people, but how am I to know that you are sent by Allah? How am I to be sure that I may trust in what you say?"

I spoke the following: "All right. Mehmet. I understand what you have just said. Knowing that you dealt in caravans and trading, it is natural that you distrust one and all, upon meeting them, and you choose your friends carefully. I shall make a deal with you which you cannot refuse. I have no control over what the Creator may do, just as no other mortal has. However, I sometimes can communicate with Ayl, who is your Allah, and get some kind of results. If there is a sign which appears which no person can make or fashion and is truly miraculous to one's senses, will you then believe us?"

Mehmet smiled. "I have seen humans bewitch asps, and make them sway. I have seen people manipulate their hands so that objects they hold seem to vanish. Those are not miraculous acts. In order for me to believe, I must see something which no person could ever do. That is my answer to you."

I thought to myself that this was the farthest I could go with rational and logical speech. Something more was needed, something spectacular, and, so, I muttered, "Well, it's up to you again, Ayl Elyon, oh master of the Universe, Creator of creation, Number-one miracle maker. I leave it up to you."

The heat was oppressive and, of course, it was a cloudless sky. The sun was high above us. Then, Ayl came through once more, as I had known he would. There was a crack of lightning, a boom of thunder, and a cloud suddenly appeared above our tree — one solitary cloud just big enough for one tree. It started to pour rain as if a storm of great power was sweeping through the town, yet outside our circle under the tree, we could see the sun still shining as before. I looked up and said aloud, "Thank you, Ayl. Once more you have shown your power. I think we have had enough rain for now."

The rain stopped instantly. Mehmet looked at us, and we could see that his dark eyes were wide open and that his mouth was gaping.

"I shall listen to you and to your advice, my friends. There is no doubt that you speak the truth. What have you to say to me? How should I be henceforth? Tell me. I shall be still."

I tried not to look smug and put on my humble face, eyes down. You see, in the short time we had been here, I had found out that women were seen but seldom heard. Men had many wives, but there was no such thing as women having many husbands. This seemed to me, to be an anomaly. After all, as I understood Creation, all human beings were created in Ayl's image. It was not the body which personified image, but the mind. Oh, well — no use trying to explain this to someone who had little background in history, or knowledge of people, or the law of Hillel, so I decided to proceed slowly.

"Mehmet, I have not come to change you into something which you are not. I am not Ayl, but only a messenger. I will try to give you the message as best I can. You will forgive me, if I stumble, and, if I say something which is not understandable, please interrupt me, and either Nahyim or I will correct or explain what I have said. That being understood, I think we should lunch, sleep through the heat of the day, and get together just before dusk and talk then."

Mehmet looked as if he were impatient to start but checked himself and agreed to meet with us later. As he assented to the meeting, we all were delighted to see a circle of colors — a complete rainbow circle, above our tree, and I commented that it was probably a sign that Ayl was satisfied thus far. Mehmet just stared in wonder, and Nahyim and I walked back to our room, leaving Mehmet sitting on the blanket, cross legged with his chin cupped in his hand, thinking.

On the way back to the house, I asked Nahyim, "You remember when you last saw a beautiful rainbow a long time ago? Now you understand how beautiful art is created and not made. Just like Ayl, it comes suddenly and appears in a burst of splendor. When you make something of leather and make a pretty design, which you have seen before, that is the process of creating, but my darling, sweet man, when we had our children, we actually created works of art! That was because we were creating in the image of Ayl. I only wish that the last step of that creation could be made a little more comfortable, and that the last stages were not so body heavy. Oh well, I guess that Ayl has ample reasons."

Nahyim, of course, roared with laughter at my philosophical ideas, and told me that I was the greatest work of art he had ever seen and that was good enough for him. And then we reached the house.

We checked on the animals and saw that they were completely contented. Camels, donkeys, chickens, ducks, goats, and sheep were all lying down and resting. It looked like a very peaceable kingdom, but, of course, the era of great art had not yet arrived.

Nahyim and I went in and snacked, for we were not very hungry, and lay down for an afternoon nap. No one was stirring because of the heat. All was quiet enough for a good rest. Before our eyes closed, we discussed how to proceed with our new friend. Should we tell him the complete history of how the Jews had founded their religion, how, after more than six hundred years after Yoshi's death, it was possible to see how it had been changed, by the introduction of the pagans into the offshoot Yoshua believer group, into a totally different system, completely divorced from its roots? If we did this, then he might think that we were telling tales about the newcomers and dismiss what we said as Aesop's sour grapes. Then, I had a bright idea. We would go to sleep after a while, for our heads needed a rest, and when we awoke we might have an answer to our problem. He looked at me with his half-closed beautiful eyes, turned to me, kissed me, turned over and promptly fell asleep. Hmmph! What a sprightly, romantic man he had become. So, I, too, slept.

We awoke later, refreshed, and noticed that there was a breeze in the air, although the heat persisted. We saw to the animals who had all become friends and paid little attention to us, and I noted that each of our lovely donkeys had found a female counterpart with which to picnic on the grass. I was truly happy for Yofi and patted him and his friend, who I named Yaffa, which means "pretty girl." Then we left them to their own thoughts, went to our meeting tree, and found Mehmet seated at his place.

Mehmet and Mission

When we greeted Mehmet, he told us that he had been thinking and wanted to tell us how he felt about our Ayl. He said that he agreed that Avraham, our patriarch, had gotten it right when he proclaimed that his Ayl was the creator of all, and that the gods or idols worshipped by others were false. But he was also worried, because Avraham's Ayl seemed to be very angry and destructive at times. It seems he had the impression that all the laws of our Torah which he had heard about seemed restrictive and of a punishing variety. His conclusion was that Allah was the same as Ayl but that, from what he had seen, the law had been changed from the original. If that were the case, then who was to know what the will of Allah really was, if we humans could change the law at will.

"I see what you mean, Mehmet. You are to be congratulated for seeing a major problem for all human beings for all times. The question is not easy to answer, for good, bad, innocent, guilty —all these things can mean different things in different situations and times. What is good to do at one time may be bad at another. It is good to cut the grain at harvest time. It is bad to do it before that. If a man steals a piece of bread from your table because his child is starving, is that bad? Compare that to a rich man who robs you. If you see someone trying to murder a child, and your sword maims that person while you are attempting to protect that child, are you guilty of a transgression?

"Understanding the law is not an easy task, and a person should study for many years before attempting to invoke the law. If you wish to teach the law, then look at what people do. Is the law for people of the town or for nomads? Is it for traders or for farmers? Is it for children, or is it for those whose understanding is mature? Those who judge must understand that the law is not a statue, which cannot be moved. The law is as a human, which must change with the times and conditions; otherwise, if change does not take place, then death appears. If it is not the death of a person, it may be the death of a city. The law must not be allowed to become like a corpse. The great sage Hillel understood this when he issued his pronouncement on the Law...."

Mehmet, who had been listening intently, suddenly interrupted, "Please stop, Mimi. Tell me about this Hillel and his explanation of the law. I do not understand how one pronouncement can explain everything"

I then told him about how Hillel had always hungered for knowledge and how this hunger had driven his learning until he had become a great and admired teacher and sage. Then I quoted to him Hillel's rule about not doing hateful things to others.

"Ah, I see now. All the laws of Ayl are meant to govern our behavior toward other humans and thus also to Allah. We measure what we do against a Rule of Gold, but is it truly worth more than 'Do unto others that which you would have them do unto you'? Why phrase it in the negative instead of the positive?"

"Ah, another deep question." said Nahyim. "Have you heard of the great thinker Hippocrates, the Greek? Clever people, those Greeks. They are to be admired for the great thinkers they produced. Hippocrates, when speaking of medicine and healing, said that the first rule to be obeyed by healers was "Do No Harm." They did not say, "Do Good." One must be careful when dealing with others that good intent should not inflict harm. One cannot know that one's good intentions are appropriate for the person, or time, or place and therefore, should hesitate before acting, to enquire of one's self if there is the possibility of harm which could result of any utterance or action.

"This is one of the most important teachings, which Ayl (Allah) wishes you to learn. If you can make that an important part of your teaching, then you will have done well for the people and for the earth. Beware though, that you speak carefully, with this in mind, that you do not use words that your followers may confuse in their minds and memories and turn your words and intentions to that which breeds argument, bitterness, and strife. Leaders have a great responsibility, and you are on the way to becoming a great leader."

"Nahyim is so right, Mehmet. Everything he says rings of truth. Every great leader sees a certain goal; however, those who follow may change those goals to something the leader never envisioned or intended. Remember — it is not all the details of your message which are the message. It is the central core, or idea of the message which must be remembered by all. Details are for scribes. Messages are for leaders. Whenever you open your mouth to speak, let the message be there, shining as a beacon, so that those who hear will follow that beacon. See, the sun is low, and the evening meal approaches. We are hungry. I believe you have heard what we have tried to bring you. What tomorrow brings, no one knows, but we must go on, and so must you. We shall accompany you to Mecca, and can assure you that you will be protected. Get a good night's sleep, for we leave after the morning meal."

"Do you mean to tell me that only three of us are going to Mecca? Why, they are just waiting to cut me up and feed me to the jackals. How can you be so sure that you can protect me? Tell me that!"

Of course, our ever-present Ayl was nigh, and no sooner had Mehmet finished his protestation than a bolt of lightning hit the top of the tree, knocking off a branch, which landed like a whiplash upon Mehmet's shoulders. We burst out laughing, while Mehmet sat stunned.

"Oh, Mehmet! Do you doubt that the Creator of all can protect you against a band of pursuers or enemies? Surely your Allah, who created all, knows how to deal with mere mortals who mean you harm. No. This is proof that you cannot doubt Allah's orders. Tomorrow we leave. I shall not even ask for your assent. That is what we shall do. Now, good night, and we shall meet after breaking the evening fast."

And Nahyim and I left, giggling as we got out of hearing, because of the look on Mehmet's face when the tree had punished him. I looked up at the evening star and said, "Oh, Ayl, you really work in wondrous ways. You treated Mehmet like a little boy and used a lowly tree to teach him a lesson about faith. That look on his face was precious. But, you must excuse us for laughing at his situation. I know how embarrassed and perplexed he must have been. But, I am sure, that, had you been in our place, you would have laughed, also. Do not blame us, for it was you who gave us the gift of humor, and, if we use it, we do so because it is ours to use."

"'In your place — in your place'? What do you mean, woman? I, the creator cannot be 'In your place.' I am Ayl. I have no body, and no appearance, and I certainly cannot be in any one 'place,' since I am omnipresent! Have I not told you that I do not wish for you to grant to me your feelings or your senses, or your perception of the Universe? I am not a human being. Get that straight — never was, am not, and never will be a human being! However, I do not blame you for the giggling, because you did an admirable job with Mehmet, and now you have to get some food and rest, because tomorrow, you finish your work here."

And there were no more words.

We ate, got up, stretched and yawned, and went to our room. As we got into bed, I asked, "Nahyim, my love, how do you feel?

"Tired and weary."

"'Tired and weary'? Do you not think that I also am tired and weary? However, I am not so tired and weary when I remember how you used to hold me and kiss me in previous days and times. Do you not think that you might save a little energy for your wife, as you go through the day? After all, you did not wed the world."

"Oh, my dear," cried Nahyim. "Never would I wish to hurt you by making you feel alone. As I looked into myself and saw how the day has affected me, I thought that you might be even wearier than I, and, so, I told you the truth. I would not want to lie to you."

I felt like picking up my sandal and knocking him on the head. Men! They are so taken up with thinking that they have no time for feelings. I took a deep breath and appealed to his reason. "Look, husband mine. I have feelings. I love you, and I know that you love me. I have a need to be held, kissed, and caressed in timely fashion. I know what you are capable of, and I want you to use that capability as much as possible. Do you understand? Am I making myself clear? Should I use other language to communicate my message?"

Nahyim said nothing. He took me in his arms, kissed me, caressed me, and later on, we slept peacefully.

Have You Ever Had a Day When Nothing Goes...

So, morning arrived when the sun appeared, as I knew it would. Do not laugh at this seemingly silly statement, for it involves a great deal of thinking. I assume that, by the time we reach a certain age, we claim to know, as a certainty, that the sun will light the sky on the next day. Yet, just because it has happened for as long as we know, what can assure us that it will continue as in past days? How do we know that tomorrow will not bring an endless darkness, with no sun, for as certain as everything we know has an end — trees, fish animals, humans — all of creation has an end, which we choose to call death. Might not the sun be destined for death? If so, when is that time to be? All fire eventually goes out and dies, into ashes and embers, and so might it not be with the sun?

So, going back to my first statement, might that statement not be my way of showing my trust in Ayl? Is it not my way of praising the continuity of creation?

Each day, the sun brings us a promise of time to come, a new chance to live a better existence, and a chance to build a better world. It is just one simple sentence, but with a universe of meaning. Oh, never mind! It was morning, and after the three of us had eaten in half-open-eyed silence, we saw to the animals. Mehmet borrowed a donkey from our hosts, and we set out for Mecca. It was a tedious journey, unmarked by oases, and the sun shone down without remorse. When we got to a large sand dune after many hours, we were able to see the city in the distance. We descended toward the city when we spied many camels. As we moved closer, we were surrounded by many fierce-looking men. They had swords, which seemed to be very sharp and curved. By now, being accustomed to this kind of behavior by some people, Nahyim and I just stopped and stared at these rowdies, who were yelling and screeching in high voices, and making quite a spectacle of themselves. Mehmet, on the other hand, just sat and trembled, hardly able to speak. Finally, we tired of staring, and, during a lull in the yelling, Nahyim called out, "We come in peace. Put away your swords, and we shall talk."

The men looked at us and laughed. One of them, close to us, yelled back, "Oh no. We hardly come in peace. We have been looking for that madman Mehmet and have found him. Not only that, but we have also found a lovely maiden who will make a lovely slave to one of us. We shall cast lots for her after we have cut you and Mehmet in bits small enough for the jackals to swallow."

I told Nahyim and Mehmet to leave it to me and to stay where they were. I urged Yofi forward toward the speaker and said to him,

"My dear man. I urge you and your group to put away the weapons and accompany us quietly into the city, for we have a message for the population. If you do not do as I ask, I am afraid for your comfort and safety. I ask you to look at us as friends who wish you no harm. See. I carry no sword, no shield, and no knife. But, be warned. I am under the protection of a power greater than you have ever known, and I do not wish you to suffer. Please make those swords vanish from sight."

He eyed me and shouted, "Know then, who is powerful. I am a son of the family of priests charged with seeing to the Kaaba. I am destined to be a priest, and thus am holy. You are a woman, and you dare to order me as if I were a child. We shall see about that! Meanwhile, make way, for we are about to do away with two vermin and take possession of three donkeys and a woman."

He turned and commanded the men to rush at Nahyim and Mehmet, and, as they were beginning their charge, there was the bolt of lightning, which blinded all of us for a moment. When we could see, the men were standing in the sand, and their camels had disappeared from under them. Looking around, we could see, far off in the distance toward the city, that the camels were almost at the city gates, but how they had gotten there was a mystery. I looked at the man in charge and spoke further.

"I ask you again as I asked you before. Put away your weapons lest misfortune befall you."

"By the last hairs of my beard, I shall never do a woman's bidding," he shouted. "I would rather die here and now than bow before you."

He came running at me, stumbled, and fell down. He got up and fell once more before he even moved. He looked perplexed, but, holding his sword, he started crawling at me.

I got off Yofi, and said to all the men with him,

"I warn you all. If he so much as comes within an arm's length of me, all of you shall enter the city in shame, for you shall be bereft of your clothing and shall return to your dwellings not only dressed as you were at the moment of birth, but also burnt by the sun. Now contemplate what I have said."

He crawled a bit more and then collapsed completely. The men milled around, talking to one another. Then one of them spoke up and said, "I do not know who or what you are. For all I know, you are a djinn, or some other spirit or even a goddess. We have decided that we shall go back to the city and not bother with the three of you. But we tell you that the people of Mecca, and especially the priests of the Kaaba, are fed up with Mehmet and his talk of his Allah and his disdain for the gods of our people. We cannot guarantee his safety."

I assured them that we did not hold them responsible for his safety, since a higher power was responsible for that. Then I shooed them off, for they had a good hour's walk in the sun in order to get to the shelter of the city. Meanwhile, we rode along, following at a leisurely pace, while we explained to Mehmet what "being protected" really meant. He was impressed. In fact, he was so impressed that he said nothing and just stared straight ahead. I wondered what thoughts he was seeing. Oh, well, it was really none of my business, but I knew that this event had made a great impression on him.

When we arrived, within a few moments of entrance, I counseled Mehmet again, saying, "Now, I know that you cannot remember all that I have told you right now, but you can remember the following: When you speak to the crowd, speak slowly, distinctly, and aiming at that one person. Also, always keep in mind the rule of Hillel. Do not get too wrapped up in explaining new laws and such. Keep it simple, so that even children may understand what you say. But first, get yourself some trusty scribes who will write down what you have said; otherwise, your efforts will be in vain. Believe me when I tell you that, unless it is done while you speak, your words will not matter in the future. We will try to be with you so that you know you have friends nearby. When we are sure that you have been once more accepted into your clan, we will then leave, for we have other Kebab to pierce. Are you prepared to take up your work, Mehmet?"

He looked at me, once more with assurance, and said, "I know what I must do. Let me see if I cannot find some of my kinsmen to act as scribes. Then, when I have told them their tasks, I shall begin speaking again, with a different message than before. Should I be too busy to speak at length with you later, I should like to thank you now, not only for my life but for the lessons and the kindness you have shown me. You have made your ancestors proud, and served them and your god, and I am beholden to you as long as I live." He bade me "Salaam" and trotted off on his donkey.

As I saw him leave, I yelled to him, "Don't forget, Mehmet. Return the donkey to my kinsmen in Yatrib. Do not forget their gracious welcome."

He waved when he heard my voice and disappeared into the waning sunset.

I wondered if he would succeed in his attempt to bring god to his people. There were some doubts lingering in my mind, concerning his incomplete knowledge which he had of our Torah, and the additional writings of those who ruled over the empire of the Romans and Byzantines. Well, only time would tell. Nahyim and I decided to try to find a place to sleep. Within a moment, we found an imaret with a spare room and an enclosed space for the animals. For a small fee, we hired the inn keeper's son to wash the donkeys, feed and water them, and make them a nice soft, straw bed on which to sleep. We ate and, feeling very weary, went to our room and slept, without bothering with conversation.

Morning came early. Well, it did not come early, for it comes whenever the sun appears. I meant that we were sorry that there was not more time to sleep, but we had made plans to return to Yatrib (which, much later, became known as Medina) and rest there a while. We set out after the morning meal and left in plenty of time, so as to arrive in Yatrib by sunset. We found later that this was not to be.

We had not gone far on our trip when the donkeys both stopped. They would not move. We cajoled and stroked, but they stood as stone statues. We did not know what to do, so, taking their reins in our hands, we started walking, but, again, they would not be moved.

Then I understood.

We Ride Into the Sunset

I told Nahyim to stop his efforts while we had a conference. There was something nagging at me. Yofi had never acted like this. I told Nahyim that Ayl wanted something from us. We were to do something. I knew not what. Finally I asked aloud,

"All right, Ayl Elyon, God of all, Creator of the Universe, grantor of life, and other things. What is it now? This is the subtlest message received thus far, and I am too simple to understand. I am sure that you do not wish us to settle in the desolate place on which we stand. It appears that you do not wish us to be in Yatrib, so what is it? Why are you silent? Just go ahead and tell us your wish, and we shall do it. Have we not been faithful servants? Why play this game with us? Come on. Be serious. Just tell us what you want us to do. That's all we ask."

As I finished, three beautiful, tall, and shady palm trees appeared before us. Under them we could see rugs, pitchers, and food. The donkeys moved toward the trees, as did we, and we sat comfortably, while the donkeys grazed on the grass, which had also appeared under the shade. We still did not know what was going on.

And then came a laughing voice, saying, "Yes, Mimi, your Lord moves in mysterious ways, although, moving is not quite the correct word. I am omnipresent and so do not have to move. Don't forget that. It is a handy saying when you don't understand something. It really doesn't have anything to do with the law or anything else. It's just as handy as any other verbal trope."

I was losing patience. "Look!" I said. "If I need humor, I shall play games with my husband. When I deal with you, Ayl, I expect you to treat me seriously. I gave up growing old with my mother and family. Nahyim and I are no longer of the world we were born into. I appreciate that you are the Lord of Humor as well as of Creation, but my God, can't you at least play with us when we are at leisure and not doing work or in the middle of a trek? We are only human, and our minds do not bounce all over the place at one time. I'm sorry if I seem ungrateful or impatient, but that's how I feel right now."

"All right, Mimi. All right. I shall now be serious with you. I appreciate, once more, your directness and your honesty. As I have told you before, you were the perfect choices for an extremely hard career. I do not have a job for you right now, because I have to wait and see what choices the followers of Yoshua, and the followers of Mehmet will make. Yoshua, it seems, did a very good job of speaking Hillel's message, but since no one wrote it down as he spoke, people had to depend on memory and folklore. Then the pagans joined the group and added their ideas. As of now, it is hard to know what they really believe and how they will turn out, even though they have written down what they think the message was. Mehmet's followers are the unknown piece of a large puzzle, and we have to wait. I shall give them time to sort themselves out, and, so, I have decided that you two will have some time off for a long vacation and then another long, restful sleep. The reason I stopped the donkeys was so that you would not turn to the right and then go north. I have chosen a spot for you, not far from here, again on the shore of a great body of water, where you shall relax and then sleep, until I once more need you. All your needs will be taken care of, and you will not be bothered with problems. Turn toward the west and travel for no longer than a day, and you will come to your nesting spot. You will recognize it when you get there. Have a good time. I'll be in touch. Now go. "There was once again silence.

We mounted the donkeys and didn't even have to pull on the reins, because they turned to the west and as we traveled. We could look backward and see that the tracks we left were a perfect straight line.

The next day, we saw, in the distance, a great sea, and, as we neared it, we saw an oasis with date palm trees, a well, a tent, and a lovely large patch of green grass for the two animals. What a lovely spot! The first thing we did was shed our clothing and run into the water, and to our surprise, the water was warm and comfortable. There were rocks of different hues at the very bottom of the clear water, and we could see all kinds of colorful fish swimming and darting about. It was just heavenly to lie on one's back and float, watching the few clouds pass by, and hear the sounds of the birds as they swooped over the water, looking for food. Every once in a while a bird would dive into the water and come up with a fish in its mouth and fly away with it, probably to feed its mate or youngsters. It made me think of the family which Nahyim and I had borne and nurtured, and I clung to my memories with mixed feelings. It is hard to be of many years, to be old feeling inside, yet young outside. I had aged very little, and my body was still something to be proud of, with very little fat, and just a few wrinkles if one looked hard enough, except that only one person in this world had permission to look. Oh, well, no use crying over spoiled mulch, as some of our farmers used to say.

After our swim, we went back to our tent and looked at the brand- new clean clothes which awaited us. After dressing, we sat down on the rugs and ate as if we were royalty. There were meats and vegetables and fruits and cool water and flasks of Yahyin, which is that miraculous gift of liquid made from grapes, which affects one's head in strange ways, if taken in excess. There were light cakes made with sweet honey. Life was good. After eating, we lay down on the grass, under the palms, and spoke of all the travels, adventures, and marvels we had experienced. In recounting them, we concluded that we could not see the results of our "messaging." As we looked back, we could not have noticed that the behavior of people had changed, and all we had heard of news from faraway lands, as told to us by traders and caravan masters, indicated that most people were not making the choices which would produce a better world. Ayl had rested on the Shabbat, the seventh day, and then had told humanity that it had the responsibility for perfecting the job of creation. That was the reason we human beings had appeared in the course of the world's development. There had been other kinds of creatures, which had "ruled the earth" but had failed to create, and, now, it was our turn.

Yet there was no evidence that human beings had heeded the call. They had dominion over the earth and its creatures. They had the law. They had an explanation of the law, which was understandable to all, yet they did not heed the still, small voice. Nahyim and I had tried our best to spread the message, and now all we could do is wait, along with Ayl, to see what humanity would do with that message. But then a new thought made itself known. I had thought before that the creatures who had come before had not created; however, later on, I found that they had. Their very deaths had enriched the soil, and I later learned that, trees, vegetation, and everything which died went back into the soil or sea and was changed into something else which was useful for future generations of creation. As I looked out at this serene earth, I could hardly envision all that was going on around me constantly. Even at moments of deep silence, there were great changes happening below the ground, in the waters, and in the air, and we humans were all part of this constant change. At this point, my head complained of fatigue, so I fell asleep.

And so we spent the next three months bathing, sunning, walking along the shore, riding our donkeys in order to give them a change of scenery. They do get bored with looking at the same grass, the same tent, day after day. They need stimulation, just as we do. At the end of the three months, we were sitting, watching the sun set over the sea, when Ayl contacted us. As I heard our names called, I knew what to expect, and it was with a feeling of regret mixed with anticipation that I answered the call. I would not know, really, how to feel until the next assignment was explained.

"Well, my able servants, I hope you have enjoyed your sojourn by the beautiful sea. You certainly earned your vacation. But now you must prepare for another sleep from which you shall not awake for quite a while, if one measures time by the heavens. For you, it will seem only as one night, but you will awake in a changed world. I, as yet, do not know what decisions will be made by the peoples who will come and go during this time, but your future work will be determined by what the world is like when you awaken. Trust in me. I shall protect and care for you while you rest. Enjoy yourselves for today, for your long sleep begins tonight. I bid you a restful sleep and sweet dreams. I can assure you that your dreams will not be anything else but sweet. That is being arranged as you hear these words. So, Mimi and Nahyim, may you be blessed with health and happiness today and as long as you live, and that is the word for today. Shalom V'Lyla Tov."

I raised my hand and waved it, saying, "Thank you, Ayl, for all your past and present gifts, for your kindness, your patience, and your protection. No other human beings have been as fortunate as your two servants. You are the sweetest god to have ever been worshipped by humans, and we are glad that you are ours."

At that moment, the donkeys, who had been grazing idly, came close to us and both attempted to speak. I knew what their noise was all about, and so I began singing the song they loved, and then they joined in, braying along with me.

Praise God, Praise God,
Praise him with drum and cymbals
Praise him with harp and kazoo,
Let all of our souls praise God
Let all of our souls praise God.

Yofi then gave me a big, wet lick-kiss right across my face. I hugged him back, and the two of them went off, lay themselves down in the grass, and contentedly fell asleep. I looked at Nahyim and said, "Well?"

"Ah, yes. That tone of voice commands an answer. That 'well' is very deep and it holds much meaning. So come, and let us bathe before the sun sets, and then we can eat and afterwards who knows, maybe we can do better than 'well'."

But I knew, and he knew, and we were both content with each other and our lives. The water was warm, the air was sweet, the food was ready, and, later on, so were we. Ah, it is good to have a man around the house.

And so later, we slept.

POSTSCRIPT

Although this concludes The First Book of Mimi, the long journey ahead for Mimi, her beloved husband Nahyim, and their loyal donkey Yofi has barely begun. The second book in this series, take this trio to many exotic places, Florence, Wittenberg, Amsterdam and Spain. Should I survive, the third volume will take them up to the 21st century in the USA. (I'm looking forward to that!)

The idea for this trip of Mimi's came from a posting I did on care2.com/ during a discussion of the "war on women" (around March/April 2012). There were some males who were posting messages which were demeaning and disparaging. I knew that a rational, straightforward answer would make no impression on them. And I imagined a prophet of old, a prophet left out of the canon — a female — who was feminine, strong, witty and articulate. I imagined her speaking as if she were addressing these males with a "Thus saith the Lord...." attitude. What would she say? Well, the Lord spoke about creating man AND woman in the image of God, giving people free will to choose between right and wrong, and chastising men for trying to enslave women.

The posting received quite a few stars and quite a few comments. One comment, in particular, I remember as telling me that this Mimi was a great commentary and suggested that she would make a great subject for a novel. Later that day, it struck me that, although I was 81 years of age, I had written many essays in college and lectures for the 8 years I had spent teaching at a University's All Life Learning Program, I had never written a novel. I notified the University that I was taking a leave of absence, cancelled my next course, and started to work during the latter part of April 2012.

I finished the first draft on the morning of July 5th 2012 and turned my attention to my one and only ever wife of 54 years, whom I had turned into a nervous and jealous woman because I had ignored her need to have me with her and had spent my time worrying about this other woman, Mimi. Imagine — I was 81 and had a jealous wife! I wish to thank Barbara for her patience and love. She is still in our home and has not shed me, and, for that, I am beholden to her.

I should also like to thank the woman from Australia who suggested that I write Mimi's story. I do not know this woman's name, but she did act as my muse-for-a-day. Thank you, whoever you are. I should also like to thank the people who run care2.com. It is one of the few sites which covers news, events, and happenings in the world which are important and which result in action by a worldwide network of concerned people who do not mind the few crackpots, trolls, and naysayers - people who post and try to insult them. The majority of these posters, regardless of political affiliation, are really into the job of perfecting this world for the future. Bless them all.

Daniel Aldouby

ABOUT THE AUTHOR

Daniel Aldouby was born in 1931 and lived about ten years overseas. His early years were spent in Tel-Aviv (1930s) and about four and one-half years in England (Leeds and London). He has also traveled extensively throughout Western Europe and the Middle East. He has a BA from Rutgers University and a Master's Degree from Temple University. His teaching experience includes thirty years in a Public School system teaching History, English, and Computer Literacy. He is also a Reading Specialist. He taught in his Congregation's afternoon and Sunday school for twenty years. His military experience consisted of four years in the USAF. After retirement, he taught for a number of years at the Osher-Rutgers University All-Life Learning Center, presenting courses in Middle East History and The History of Religion. During his escapes from winter in Bucks County PA, he attends Florida Atlantic University, All Life Learning School. He is still a student. Presently, he is on leave of absence from Rutgers University OSHER- RUALL while he finishes the *Mimi* trilogy. Much of the content of these tales, results from questions asked by Dan and his students, during his teaching career.

Made in the USA
Charleston, SC
20 July 2014